P9-DHJ-007

NEB

The *Brain*

Finds a Leg

The

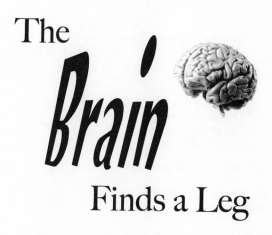

Brain

Finds a Leg

Martin Chatterton

PEACHTREE

ATLANTA

Published by
PEACHTREE PUBLISHERS
1700 Chattahoochee Avenue
Atlanta, Georgia 30318-2112
www.peachtree-online.com

Text © 2009 by Martin Chatterton

First published in Australia by Little Hare Books in 2007
First United States edition published in 2009 by Peachtree Publishers

All rights reserved. No part of this publication may be reproduced, stored
in a retrieval system, or transmitted in any form or by any means—
electronic, mechanical, photocopy, recording, or any other—except for
brief quotations in printed reviews, without the prior permission of the
publisher.

Cover design by Maureen Withee
Book design by Melanie McMahon Ives

Printed in the United States of America
10 9 8 7 6 5 4 3 2 1
First Edition

Library of Congress Cataloging-in-Publication Data
Chatterton, Martin.
  The Brain finds a leg / written by Martin Chatterton. -- 1st ed.
      p. cm.
  Summary: In Farrago Bay, Australia, thirteen-year-old Sheldon is recruited
by a new student, Theo Brain, to help investigate a murder, which is tied
not only to bizarre animal behavior but also to a diabolical plot to alter
human intelligence.
  ISBN 978-1-56145-503-4 / 1-56145-503-2
  [1. Mystery and detective stories. 2. Intellect--Fiction. 3. Animals--Habits
and behavior--Fiction. 4. Inventions--Fiction. 5. Schools--Fiction. 6. Aus-
tralia--Fiction. 7. Humorous stories.] I. Title.
  PZ7.C3915Br 2009
  [Fic]--dc22
                        2009000304

J F CHA
 1716 5088   12/3/13   NEB
Chatterton, Martin.

The Brain finds a leg
     ABJ

To everyone at Byron Bay Soccer Club
(even Debbie)

LeRoy Collins Leon Co.
Public Library System
200 West Park Avenue
Tallahassee, FL 32301

The Bit at the Beginning...

*A*wooooooclicktocktockclickwoooooclick!"

Infinity Override stood Titanic-style at the prow of *The Coreal,* her handwoven poncho billowing out behind her as the boat headed along the river toward postcard-perfect Farrago Bay. Beaming meaningfully at the water, she placed her hands together as if in prayer and made a noise like she'd caught her knuckle on a cheese grater.

"Awooooo-eeeeeticktick-eeeeeaaaaahwooooo!"

The revolting screech, Captain McGlone knew from previous whale-watching trips Infinity had taken on his boat, was the sound of her singing to the humpbacks. Her voice scraped against McGlone's ears like a careless dentist's drill catching an exposed root, and his fingers curled temptingly around a nearby spanner. No, he couldn't do it, not even to Infinity. She was, after all, a paying customer, silly name or no silly name. McGlone felt that changing your name to something weird should be punishable by a slap in the face with a large wet fish.

He turned away from Infinity and clicked on the boat's intercom microphone.

"Good morning, everyone," he said, his voice heavy with electronic hiss. "This is your captain speaking. I'd like everyone to put on their life vests now, please; we're coming out of the river soon and it's going to get a little bumpy. Sorry the vests don't look very attractive, folks, but the coastguards prefer me not to drown more than, say, two or three of you each trip."

McGlone slipped *The Coreal* expertly through the narrow, treacherous channel that cut between the high rocky arms of the surrounding cliffs as the passengers, thirty-one in total, chattered excitedly and struggled into their life vests. Once in open water, the crosscurrents and waves of the ocean met the outpouring of the river and more than a few of them began to regret signing up for the whale-watching trip.

Not Infinity Override.

"It's a spiritual experience," she said earnestly to her skinny, bearded companion, a part-time crystal healer called DJ Love who was, Captain McGlone was pleased to note, beginning to look a little green.

Twenty minutes later, *The Coreal* was long past the river mouth and out into the darker blue of true ocean. McGlone eased up on the throttle as they came to the first good whale spot of the day. He let *The Coreal* drift with the current.

DJ Love began throwing up his morning muesli (with extra yogurt, by the look of it).

"Get it all out, brother," said McGlone happily as he passed, slapping him on the back. "Better out than in."

DJ Love groaned and turned his clammy face back to the water.

McGlone chuckled and lifted his binoculars. Today was looking up.

Below the boat in the perfect blue bay, about a kilometer from shore, something large and purposeful was moving toward *The Coreal*. More than fifteen meters from snout to tail, the lead humpback weighed close to forty tons. She had travelled more than four thousand miles in the past five months, in a loose pod of eight to ten whales. The whale knew all about the boat on the surface, having been in Farrago Bay for almost two weeks. There was something about the water here the whales liked.

Something different.

"Hey, Skipper!" yelled a passenger. "We actually going to *see* any whales on this whale-watching trip?"

"Sure, sure," said McGlone, squinting at the water. "Guaranteed, as always."

The pod was right where he knew it would be. And that was the problem, he thought, scratching his chin. Every year the whales moved steadily north or south, depending on the time of year, never really staying in one spot for too long. Why had this group remained?

McGlone eased *The Coreal* closer and lifted the microphone.

"Um, folks, if you look out over the port beam—that's the left-hand side of the ship—you'll see some whales."

There was, as always, a satisfying murmur of "oohs" and "aahs" as the first whale broke the surface a few hundred meters away, in full breach. It was a glorious sight. The gray and white whale rolled onto its side and smashed one giant fluke into the blue water again and again, each splash raising a chorus of wonder from the tourists.

"Can't we get any closer?" whined a spotty kid with dreadlocks. "I thought we were gonna see them, you know, up close and personal."

McGlone slid *The Coreal* a shade closer. A few more meters wouldn't harm anyone. Everywhere you looked the telltale spumes of the whales erupted as they exhaled loudly. Today was a real bonanza—the whales so close the passengers could almost reach out and touch them.

"Uh, these guys are *very* close now, Skipper," said a nervous-looking man in a yellow windbreaker. As he spoke, a big humpback crested out of the water, so near *The Coreal* that its splash sent spray flying clear across the deck.

There was a chorus of nervous laughter and, despite his instinctive disregard for anything the passengers said, McGlone found himself agreeing. The whales *were* close.

Too close.

On the starboard side, another humpback broke free of the surface and splashed *The Coreal* heavily again. The boat rocked from side to side, and this time some of the passengers let out little yelps of alarm.

"I think it might be wise to back off a little," said McGlone, reaching for the throttle. "Don't want anyone getting too wet!"

He steered *The Coreal* away, allowing himself a small sigh of relief as clear water opened up between the boat and the nearest visible humpback. He was just beginning to wonder if he was getting soft, when there was a loud bump and *The Coreal* shuddered like it had hit solid rock. One or two of the tourists screamed.

Sweet Davy Jones, thought McGlone, what the hell was *that*?

Another sudden bang followed immediately from right below the bridge, and *The Coreal* shook violently from stem to stern. Almost before anyone had a chance to react, a monstrous black and gray tail rose from the water and smashed down onto the deck. Wood splintered as the railing collapsed, and two panic-stricken tourists scrambled away from the gaping hole.

Behind the boat, another humpback rolled lazily on the surface, its eye clearly visible as *The Coreal* tipped crazily forward. Infinity Override, frozen in her *Titanic* position at the prow, toppled slowly toward the water, her mouth open in surprise. A humpback calf picked her up on one massive fluke and flipped her as casually as a rubber toy, clean over *The Coreal*.

"Infinity!" squealed DJ Love as she sailed over the boat, her flowing clothes streaming out behind her.

Infinity looked down at him helplessly as she passed, before splashing down hard into the ocean. Her poncho snagged on the gnarled fluke of a nearby humpback, which took off, Infinity in tow.

"*Awoooooaaaaarrrgh!*" she wailed, although no one thought she was singing to the whales this time. As the whale dipped below the water, Infinity's cries stopped with a horrible glugging sound.

There was silence for a moment and then full-scale panic broke out as *The Coreal* started to rise, stern first, out of the water.

"They're lifting us!" screamed a fat woman in an orange dress, clinging to a lanyard. "Oh my God, they're lifting us!"

She was right.

McGlone couldn't believe it. He'd never seen any-thing like this before. No one had. Humpbacks just flat out *didn't do this.* McGlone had heard of a few rare accidental collisions between the whales and spotter boats from time to time, but this was something on another level.

McGlone lurched toward the side of the boat and looked over. Three of the humpbacks, packed tight in together, hoisted *The Coreal* like she was made from balsa before dropping her heavily into the ocean, almost cracking the boat in two. McGlone crunched back heav-ily into the control panel, a large gash opening on his head. A second massive impact followed quickly from the starboard side and then another from the port.

The boat was being systematically smashed to pieces by the whales.

With a sudden, final crack the sides of the vessel splintered and then broke. Cold water poured in and *The Coreal* began to slip below the surface fast.

"Abandon ship!" yelled McGlone, as screaming passengers leapt overboard.

The spotty tourist with the dreadlocks disappeared under the surface before rising up again, wild-eyed and spluttering. A young adult humpback picked him up by his hair and swung him from side to side in slow, lazy arcs before flicking him casually into the ocean. A few seconds later the tourist bobbed up and began swimming as fast as he could away from the whales. It seemed everyone had the same idea. The problem was doing it.

Two tourists disappeared straight into the mouth of the biggest whale right in front of McGlone. The whale spat them out again like a cat spitting out a hairball. The tourists screamed something in Japanese, hit the water, and began swimming away from the carnage. Everywhere McGlone looked it was pandemonium.

The chubby woman in orange was being tossed between two whales like a volleyball. DJ Love swam around in little circles, his head high above the water.

"Infinity!" he shouted, his voice now high-pitched and shaking with fear. "Infinity! Infinity! Where are you Infinity? Sing to them Infinity! Sing for your life! Communicate, baby, communicate!"

There was no reply. McGlone didn't hold out much hope for poor old Infinity, whale songs or no whale songs. Suddenly DJ Love rose from the water, sitting on the back of a whale. Frozen with fear he clung onto the whale's blowhole as it headed straight out to the horizon. To Infinity and beyond.

McGlone had seen enough. It was every man and woman for themselves. He struck out purposefully toward the shore as *The Coreal* finally gurgled below the surface. McGlone increased his speed with grim determination, the screams of the tourists fading behind him as he fought the panic that made his breath come in ragged bursts. Arms like lead, lungs on fire. Just concentrate on each stroke. Don't think. Just *do.* Come on, man! Keep going. It might be all right. It *might.*

One hundred meters, two hundred meters.

By his reckoning he had swum almost three hundred meters and was beginning to feel he might have slipped away, when he felt the water shift underneath him. Below, the largest of the humpbacks slid past in a blur of dark shadow and controlled power.

McGlone stopped swimming, looked down at the huge black shape underneath him and knew what was coming. There was something almost poetic about it.

He looked around at the clean sweep of the bay he knew so well. Here, away from the wreckage of *The Coreal,* there was silence. It was crazy; he could see the town bobbing in and out of his vision on the rise and fall of the swell. Only that short, impossible distance away, people were going about the everyday life of Farrago Bay—drinking coffee, gossiping at The Pig, buying groceries, sunbathing—while *this* was going on out here.

McGlone was not a religious man but he lifted his eyes up to the sky.

Directly in front of him the surface of the sea lifted in a ball, and then exploded as forty tons of humpback leapt clear of the water in an incredible display of power and energy. Like the slow-motion footage of a rocket being launched into space, a million diamond stars of foam spattered outwards and upwards as the whale reached the top of its leap. For an instant McGlone looked up, awestruck even in his final moments, at the sheer scale of the beast arcing back toward him. He almost wept at the utter majesty of it as the whale blotted out the sun.

He closed his eyes and thought of his sons, his wife, his life.

And then he thought of nothing.

Chapter 1

Two years and one day after *The Coreal* disaster, Captain McGlone's youngest son, Sheldon, was woken by a gang of vicious goblins prying open his eyelids with vinegar-coated claws and pounding a sharpened spike of white-hot metal into the top of his head. Even Sheldon, who had seen plenty of horror movies, had to admit this didn't seem likely, but he could have sworn it was *exactly* what was happening to him that Tuesday morning.

He groaned and, with the infinite care of a bomb-disposal expert in a firework factory, cracked open an eyelid. It hurt. Some time passed before Sheldon had the will to make another attempt.

"C'mon dude," he croaked, "time to show a bit of grit. You are thirteen after all. Grow *up!*"

Sheldon pushed his chest out manfully and felt a tiny swelling of bravery. He could cope with this, he *could*. What on earth had happened to reduce him to this state? A car crash? A nuclear war?

By now he was half-convinced he would open his

eyes and see the fluorescent glare of a hospital emergency room and the face of a kindly doctor telling him a particularly tender part of his anatomy had been whipped off.

The image shook Sheldon into action.

With a superhuman effort he raised his head up from his pillow, forced his reluctant eyes open and tried to squint some meaning into his surroundings.

Oh sweet relief! Not the emergency ward after all, but the reassuring mess of his own small bedroom. Sheldon relaxed a little and struggled into a semi-upright position, one hand cradling the front of his head as last night came flooding back.

The sugar binge. Ouch.

Empty marshmallow packets drifted around the bedroom like overgrown confetti. Drifts of chocolate wrappers lay feet deep against the walls. Two super-sized Slurpee-Freez buckets ("cups" wasn't really a big enough word) rolled lazily across the floor. They jostled for position with candy-crunch crumbs, sugar-bomb fragments, and the debris from what looked like an explosion at a chocolate factory. A half-chewed family bar of fudge lay on the floor collecting stray hair and dust balls.

Fudge! I don't even *like* fudge, thought Sheldon. Fudge was the stuff that grannies ate, wasn't it?

With a groan he caught sight of the remains of his mother's gift box of assorted chocolate liqueurs. A vague memory of scarfing down fistfuls of miniature chocolate-bottles filled with vile liquids that tasted of medicine jumped into Sheldon's mind. *That* was what had done the real damage. A whole box of chocolate liqueurs. Bad idea.

Sheldon binged when he was unhappy and last night he had been, no question, the unhappiest he could remember since Dad died. "Lost at sea." That was how they'd put it when they finally called off the search parties. Three little words hiding the story: four dead and a boatload of deranged tourists washed ashore gibbering about humpback whales attacking like wolves. Two years had gone by since then and no one was any nearer understanding what had happened out there.

Sheldon lay back and tried to clear his head. It promised to be a difficult task. As the summer rain began to batter down on the corrugated-tin roof, Sheldon sighed. He sighed a lot these days.

What a life. What a stinking miserable excuse for an existence, thought Sheldon. What was the point of even getting out of bed?

Then he brightened as he thought of something. At least it wasn't a school day.

"SHEL-DON!" wailed his mother from downstairs. "Get up, you're late for school!"

Life sucks, thought Sheldon and pulled the covers back over his head.

Chapter 2

Seventy-two extremely unpleasant minutes later, Sheldon was sitting at his usual place in school feeling as low as a slug in a limbo contest, when a small lump of saliva-soaked paper hit the back of his head.

He didn't respond. What was the point? It would only enrage Fergus Feebly, Sheldon's repulsive, ginger-headed tormentor, and encourage his small gang of mental midgets into an even greater frenzy of spit-balling.

Instead, Sheldon opted to ignore the spitballs as a silent, dignified rebuke to his attackers. Sheldon also held out a slim hope that if he ignored Feebly and didn't brush the wet paper off, Feebly might lose heart, examine his actions closely, feel really bad about what he was doing, start weeping, explode with shame, and die a nasty, horrible, gory death right here in front of everyone, ending his reign of terror in Class 8C once and for all.

It didn't happen of course; things like that never do, do they?

Sheldon looked gloomily toward Miss Fleming, his English and homeroom teacher, for some moral support. Wasn't she supposed to be on the lookout for nasty little scumbuckets like Feebly?

The short answer, as always, was "no."

Sheldon didn't really expect help from her. Fleming had only been at the school for two years, but to Sheldon she was as much a part of the building as the desks—and he'd had no more protection from Fleming than he'd had from the desks. Sheldon sometimes thought that if Fergus Feebly decided one day to roast him over an open fire in her class, Fleming would just shift her chair closer to warm her hands.

And what big hands they were. They looked like they'd be more at home at the end of the arms of a lumberjack. Fleming was a tall woman of the kind usually described as big-boned. To Sheldon she looked like she'd been badly assembled in a Taiwanese factory that specialized in making overlarge, rubbery-skinned, astonishingly ugly action dolls of middle-aged female psychopaths.

A slurping noise came from behind Sheldon's left ear. Past experience told him that the enemy were about to launch another possibly fatal attack using a spitball the size of Neptune. Sheldon had just tensed his neck muscles into no-flinch mode when the classroom door opened and in walked a new boy.

A ripple of excited chatter swept across the classroom.

"Silence!" barked Fleming in her slightly accented voice. There were moments when Sheldon thought that

Miss Fleming may have been a space alien disguised as a human; that might account for the accent.

Miss Fleming glanced at the intruder and sniffed.

For close observers of Fleming (and since survival in Farrago Bay meant keeping a very close watch on everything Fleming did, they *all* fell into that category), that sniff meant one thing and one thing only: keep your head down and say nothing. *Nada—capice?*

Supremely unaware of his fate, the new kid closed the classroom door with a soft *snik,* walked calmly to her desk, and handed her a sheet of paper.

Class 8C waited with the air of a shoal of piranhas eyeing a wading antelope.

Fresh blood.

The new arrival was short, thin, and almost ghostly white. His hair had been cut close to his scalp by a barber with blunt scissors and no sense of humor. An oversized pair of battered black-framed glasses perched on his small, unremarkable nose, lending him a somewhat owlish appearance. He wore a T-shirt with a faded picture of a scowling face printed on it, ordinary wrinkled jeans, not particularly clean, not exactly what you would call dirty. Store-brand sneakers on his feet. There was nothing very noticeable about him except perhaps for his slightly larger than average head.

"Jeez!" hissed Feebly. "What a geek!"

The new boy looked back at the class as if studying a collection of extremely uninteresting bugs. He didn't seem at all uncomfortable up there in front of everyone, thought Sheldon—not like Sheldon would have been. He didn't blush, or fidget, or hang his head, or do any of the things other people might have done in the same situation. He stared coolly back at the class, blinking occasionally, his cold eyes moving steadily around the room like a watchtower searchlight.

Sheldon looked away, unnerved.

A buzz of expectation ran through the class as they waited for Fleming's reaction. Sheldon noticed her flick a glance at the new kid and, for the briefest of moments, he thought he saw a flinch of—something—recognition, fear? As quickly as the strange expression on her face had arrived, it disappeared, her familiar scowl bolted back in place, normal service resumed. Sheldon shook his head. He must have been mistaken.

Fleming put down her pen and gave the kid her best laser-beam stare, the kind that had almost vaporized some of the toughest students at Farrago Bay High before now. Fleming's stare was a real test of backbone.

The new kid must have had a spine made of solid titanium because he returned Fleming's look without batting so much as an eyelash, never mind a whole lid. He glanced down nonchalantly at his fingernails. For an unbelievable moment Sheldon thought he might even start whistling. The alien she-beast allowed her laser-stare to linger on him for a few seconds more before flicking her eyes back down to the note he'd brought in.

"A new addition to 8C," she muttered. "Wonderful."

Miss Fleming looked up at the class.

"This," she said, smiling as sweetly as a carpet snake, "is 'The Brain,' everyone. Isn't *that* a funny name?"

Class 8C chortled dutifully in a sickening display of naked sucking up. Guiltily, Sheldon joined in.

"*Theo*, madam," said the new kid, sharply and clearly, his first words since entering the classroom. "I am afraid you are in error as regards my first name. Do not feel too critical of yourself. It is a simple mistake for people of limited intelligence to make. My name is actually *Theo*. Theo Brain. Short for Theophilus. But 'The Brain' will suffice for the moment. It has a certain ring to it. Pray excuse my interruption."

He waved his hand regally.

Behind Sheldon, Feebly sniggered snottily. "Man, oh man," he said, in a low voice brimming with glee. "Is *he* gonna get it!"

Miss Fleming's mustache bristled with indignation and she glared at the new kid as if he were something unpleasant caught under her shoe.

"Yes, dear," she said, her eyes glittering dangerously. She dripped a smile of undiluted venom in his direction, her face arranged in what passed for a pleasant expression.

It was like seeing a shark trying to smile.

"And remember, class," the teacher continued, looking knowingly at Fergus Feebly, "there is to be absolutely no bullying of The Brain, oh dear me no; there will be *no* taking him down to the back of the sports field and shoving him in the mud, for example. And definitely no dipping him headfirst down the toilets, or putting bull ants in his pants. No, we don't want anything like that at all. And some of you may be tempted to put flour in his locker, or tie his shoelaces together, or poke fun at his somewhat girly foreign accent, or 'accidentally' clip his rather large head with a sharp object as you pass. Or you might think it would possibly be funny to throw his shoes up a tree. All these things would be wrong! Do you understand?"

Fleming paused and then looked directly at Theo, her eyes gleaming behind her steel-rimmed glasses.

"Yes, madam," said The Brain. "Your meaning is perfectly clear."

Fleming turned to the class.

"Now, 8C, let's give The Brain a big Farrago Bay welcome!"

She raised her large hands and slapped them together like two slabs of meat. Class 8C clapped somewhat unenthusiastically. Miss Fleming patted The Brain hard on his head and prodded him with an iron finger toward the chair next to Sheldon.

Before the new boy moved, he leaned over and whispered something in her ear.

Fleming looked like she'd swallowed a live electric eel.

The Brain straightened up and sauntered toward his chair without a backward look. He glanced at Sheldon, nodded briefly, sat down, and produced a pipe (yes, a pipe) from his back pocket. He placed the stem between his teeth and settled back comfortably, his legs crossed at the ankles.

Miss Fleming stood up rather unsteadily, coughed, tried to speak, and failed. To Sheldon, she looked like she'd just discovered the mother ship was not returning to earth.

She produced a textbook and, in a curiously nervous voice, continued Class 8C's education with a hugely interesting look at a poem about Belgian cheese making in the fourteenth century.

Sheldon sat back, tuned out Fleming's voice, and let out a long breath. He felt like he'd been holding it since Theo had come into the classroom. Then Sheldon noticed something else.

His sugar headache had completely disappeared.

The rest of the day was the most interesting Sheldon had experienced since starting at the school. After seeing what had happened with Miss Fleming, Class 8C had a healthy respect for the new kid. Even Feebly and his collection of reject garden gnomes were wary.

When anyone spoke directly to the new kid, which wasn't often, they called him The Brain, never Theo or Ted or, for that matter, Theophilus. It just seemed the right thing to do and he never corrected anyone.

During her lesson, Fleming gave The Brain a wide berth, as you would a small but extremely venomous snake. If she did come into unavoidable direct contact with him—he corrected her spelling twice and disagreed politely with a fact or two about the role of the witches in *Macbeth*—she smiled glassily and nodded before moving on to another, easier, victim.

Sheldon watched, impressed, as The Brain sailed through the day's schoolwork with unbelievable speed. Problems that Sheldon could never solve if he lived to be a thousand years old were dispatched in seconds. The Brain *understood* algebra. He knew what a linear quadratic equation was. He could explain why planes didn't drop out of the sky. At lunchtime The Brain sat cross-legged underneath a low tree at the southern end of the oval and *read a book* as if it was fun.

Rumors about him swept through the school like an outbreak of head lice.

"My brother's girlfriend saw him getting out of a long black car on Lingside Road with two men in black suits," said Moira Twose. "I think he's a space alien!"

Nola Scully: "He eats metal!"

Alessandro Squale: "He's forty-two years old and a witness in a big Mafia trial down south. He's up here in disguise so they don't bump him off!".

"His family is a bunch of devil-worshippers out behind Coldcut Creek! They sacrifice children every full moon and he's here looking for a regular supply!" said Sheldon, who only said it to join in with the rest of them.

Whatever the truth was (and Sheldon was fairly sure it didn't involve human sacrifice, metal-eating, or Mafia trials), the wild gossip washed away like dirt on the road. The interest in The Brain gradually slackened and, by the end of the day, life had settled back into what passed for normality in Farrago Bay.

Chapter 3

Standing on his head, Carefree O'Toole looked out at an upside-down Farrago Bay spread out far below him and thought long and hard about the best way to hypnotize a spaniel. Farrago Bay's best-known pet psychiatrist and worst bongo player concentrated on his yoga breathing, his baggy lilac trousers flapping around his scrawny thighs in the breeze that blew up the hill. The morning storm had passed quickly, leaving the grass sparkling, the air charged with positive ions. A peach of a day.

Carefree O'Toole practiced his yoga and positive thinking every morning before seeing his animal clients. It helped defog what was left of his mind. Today was no exception. Beans, an eight-year-old cocker spaniel with severe depression and an eating disorder, was due in later that morning.

It was O'Toole's theory that the dog had been badly mistreated by the prime minister in a previous life. O'Toole decided to prove it with a session of hypnosis. Carefree O'Toole thought that most problems could be directly traced back to a prime minister—either the current toothy form, or a previous incarnation.

Relaxed and rejuvenated, O'Toole moved onto the *Adho Mukha Vrksasana,* which required him to balance on his head and hands, his skinny black-haired legs and bare feet sticking straight up into the blue sky. He closed his eyes, trying as always to tune out the incessant chatter of the lorikeets in the huge fig tree that stood proudly on top of the ridge.

Lorikeets, of which Farrago Bay had a gigantic number, always struck Carefree as noisy and argumentative, and today was no exception. As a caring person, Carefree knew he should embrace the wonder of Mother Nature in all her glorious forms, but somehow (although he would never admit this to anyone) he always found lorikeets to be a little...how could he put this...*lower class.* They reminded him of those hideous people from the Gold Coast. He wished they would sometimes simply *shut up.*

The lorikeets stopped chattering.

At once. All at the same time. The silence was so sudden, so unexpected, that it almost knocked O'Toole off balance. He opened his eyes and looked at the fig tree, surprised. The lorikeets *never* stopped chattering at this time of day. Still, he thought, never look a gift lorikeet in the mouth. He closed his eyes again, glad for a bit of peace.

Which was why, a few moments later, he never saw the lorikeets leave the fig tree in a single green, yellow, and red cloud numbering maybe two or three thousand birds. They swooped several times around Lookout

Point in a dense, silent flock before hovering gently into a position thirty meters above O'Toole's upturned feet.

Blissfully unaware, Carefree O'Toole breathed deeply.

In. *My.*

Out. *Mind.*

In. *Is.*

Out. *Empty.*

With one last exhalation he judged the yoga session to be over. Slowly he dropped back into a cross-legged sitting position and opened his eyes, blinking twice to adjust his vision to the light.

Something wasn't quite right.

Unless he was mistaken, everything had suddenly gotten darker. It didn't seem quite so sunny as when he had closed his eyes. He looked up to check if the storm had circled around again and yelped involuntarily as he saw the giant rainbow cloud of lorikeets hovering above him, the soft whisper of their wings as audible as a distant conversation in a cathedral. Carefree O'Toole blinked disbelievingly. *What the—?* He waved uncertainly at the birds.

"Shoo! Clear off!"

Nothing. The lorikeet cloud didn't move a centimeter. O'Toole hadn't even been sure that lorikeets *could* hover. Yet, here they were, plainly, hovering and looking like they could hover all day long. It was disturbing.

O'Toole stood up nervously, gathered his canvas bag and bongo drum, and stepped cautiously back down the path toward home. The lorikeet cloud moved with him. If he didn't know better he could have sworn the birds were following him. He stopped and looked up. The birds stopped.

He stepped two paces left. The cloud moved with him.

He stepped three paces backwards and the birds shifted position, reversing above him. Can they do that? he thought with a shock. Can birds fly backwards? Later, O'Toole thought that the flying backwards thing might have been the most frightening part of the whole weird episode.

"Now, look," he said, waving his bongo at the birds.

He never finished his sentence. With a noise like distant thunder, each and every bird simultaneously opened its bowels and dumped a monstrous cascading avalanche of snow white lorikeet poop right over Care-free O'Toole.

Chapter 4

T wo nights after The Brain had arrived at Sheldon's school there was a storm. A big one. Black as pitch and wet as it was possible to be without actually being underwater, it was a night to stay indoors. Sheldon, coughing and sneezing, had been absent from school with a summer cold. He munched glumly on a pie he couldn't taste and wished that something, anything, would happen to liven things up.

At that moment the doorbell rang.

Sheldon sat up, surprised not just by the timing of the bell but because the McGlone household had few callers after dark, especially on nights like this.

"Shel-don!" bawled Sheldon's mother over the ever-present roar from the TV set. "Can you get that? We're watching our favorite show!"

Sheldon put down the remains of his supper, pressed the Pause button on his computer game, and clumped downstairs. He switched the porch light on and opened the front door. Outside, under a dripping black umbrella, stood The Brain. He nodded briskly to Sheldon, made a kind of saluting motion, and waved his pipe.

"Good evening, Sheldon."

"Oh. Um…uh…hi," said Sheldon, brushing the pie crumbs from around his mouth.

The Brain held out his hand and Sheldon shook it uncertainly. His skin was cool to the touch, almost cold, and for a moment Sheldon considered the possibility that The Brain, along with Fleming, was an evil alien sent down from Uranus to take over the world. Maybe he was Fleming's contact agent?

"Sheldon," said The Brain. "Pray forgive the intrusion at this late hour. How is your cold? Improved, I trust?"

Sheldon grunted something meaningless while The Brain shook out his umbrella and placed it carefully in a corner of the porch. He dried his spectacles with a handkerchief and stepped through the door into the battleground that was the McGlone front room. A foul, swirling fog of cigarette smoke parted for a brief moment and revealed Sheldon's mother sitting in a faded dressing gown that might have once been blue, watching a soap. Alongside her sat her "boyfriend," the stringy-looking Sergeant Al Snook of the Farrago Bay police force.

It was Sheldon's greatest wish in life that his mother wouldn't completely lose her marbles and marry Sergeant Snook, who was, in all respects, completely unacceptable stepfather material. The man wore his hair in a comb-over, for god's sake. The thought of having Snook lumbering around the house permanently, patting him on the head and calling him sonny, was something that made Sheldon want to go and lie down for a few years in a dark room with a cold towel across his eyes. Wasn't life hard enough, without Snook joining the family?

There hadn't been a moment since Captain McGlone's death when Sheldon didn't wish his dad would walk through the door. He hadn't been the greatest dad in the world, that was true, but he was a long way from being the worst. Most importantly, he was *Sheldon's* dad.

Was, thought Sheldon with a jolt. Past tense. It was still brutal, shocking, the idea that Dad wasn't there now, farting grumpily in front of the TV and moaning about the government. What Sheldon would give to hear his dad moaning right now. Sheldon missed him. A lot. Which was, of course, the main reason he hated his mother seeing Snook. Despite a comprehensive list of reasons to dislike Snook, the real problem with Snook was that he wasn't Peter McGlone.

"Mum," said Sheldon, breaking off his train of thought, "this is, er…"

He trailed off, unsure of exactly what to call The Brain. It was a bit like introducing Spider-Man or The Green Hornet. Before Sheldon could choose between "Theo" and "a new kid from school," his mother looked up briefly, saw that a real live breathing kid had come to visit Sheldon, and performed a classic double take. Snook, a second or two behind her—his reaction time wasn't good—did exactly the same.

"Strewth, Mary!" he blurted, almost dropping his beer. "Sheldon's found a frie—*oof!*"

Mary McGlone, recovering her poise quicker than Snook, jabbed a bony elbow hard into his ribs and shot him A Look. He knew enough to keep quiet.

The Brain stepped forward into the awkward moment and took Mrs. McGlone's hand. She stabbed out her cigarette on a nearby ashtray with the other. There was always a nearby ashtray.

"Enchanted, Mrs. McGlone," said The Brain through the clouds of choking smoke. "Please do not stir yourself from your entertainment. I have some business with Sheldon that requires a degree of privacy. We won't disturb you and the sergeant any longer. He has had another hard day at Henderson's Quarry, I see. Is there an anteroom or conservatory we could withdraw to, perhaps?"

Sheldon's mother nodded vaguely, plainly transfixed by the pipe and accent of the odd-looking boy in front of her. Snook, peering suspiciously at The Brain, rubbed his ribs.

"How'd you know I've had a hard day, sonny?" said Snook, eyes narrowed in what he fondly imagined was a look of cool intelligence, but which in fact made him look like a nearsighted possum. "And, for that matter, how'd *you* know I was a sergeant, eh?"

The Brain let go of Mrs. McGlone's hand, bowed slightly to her, and turned to Snook. His round glasses reflected the blue light from the TV and hid his eyes. The effect was a little creepy.

"It is quite simple, my dear fellow," said The Brain. "Although you are not in uniform I observe you still have your police-issue shirt on underneath your sweater. That particular shade of police blue—Bodger Blue Light, if I remember correctly from a recent paper I compiled on cotton dyes—is *only* worn by members of the force in this state. Outside on the porch I noticed a large pair of black boots, size fourteen, which, in the absence of any other large-footed policemen in the area, I assumed to be yours. The label on the ankle indicated that they were made by Forces Footwear of Pitt Street in Brisbane, a company that specializes in shoes of a slightly softer and higher quality than those normally issued to mere constables. With these factors in mind I made the simple deduction that you carry the rank of sergeant."

"I could have been an inspector!" said Snook.

"Y-es…" said The Brain slowly, looking at him with the unnerving microscope stare Sheldon had first seen when The Brain had stepped into Class 8C. "I suppose that *might* have been possible. However, with your uneducated demeanor, I guessed at sergeant, and I judge from your indignation that I am correct. As to your hard day at Henderson's, that is a mere trifle. Your boots were muddied with mud formed by slate dust of a particularly individual color—Italian Blue Verona slate dust, to be precise—of a texture found at quarries. The only quarry in this area that produces Italian Blue Verona is Henderson's. From the amount of mud and the depth of the dirt on your soles I deduced you had recently spent some time there. I also see you have a beer in your hand and its empty fellow lies on the floor: a sure sign of a man having had a difficult day. Recent statistics from the International Bureau of Probability state that there is a 97.9 percent chance I am correct. My reasoning is flawless. I think you'd agree?"

There was a brief pause during which the only sounds came from the television and Snook picking his jaw up off the floor.

The Brain gestured with his pipe toward the stairs and looked at Sheldon with raised eyebrows.

"Shall we?" he said.

Once upstairs The Brain made himself comfortable. He took the only chair in the room, dropped his backpack at his feet, leaned forward, and turned Sheldon's computer off. The only sound now was the dull throb of *doof-doof* coming from Sean's room down the hallway.

The Brain fixed Sheldon with his big goggling glasses and pointed the stem of his pipe at him.

"I shan't beat around the bush as time is most certainly against us on this one, old boy," he said. "You may be pleased to learn that—from an admittedly short list of candidates—I have selected *you*!"

He sat back, a smile etched onto his moonlike face, plainly waiting to be thanked.

"*Selected?*" asked Sheldon. "For what exactly?"

"For the role of a lifetime, dear bean, the role of a lifetime."

Sheldon looked at him blankly. "Role?"

The Brain smiled again—not an altogether pleasant sight it has to be said—and jabbed the stem of his pipe in Sheldon's chest.

"Sidekick, of course," he said. "You, Sheldon, are to be my trusted sidekick!"

He sat back on the bedroom chair and replaced the pipe in his mouth, an unnerving gleam in his eye.

There was a lull. During the lull (which, as lulls go, was a pretty big lull and was threatening to become a full-scale Awkward Moment) Sheldon's bedroom door opened and Sean stuck his face around the side. The decibel level rose from the sound system vibrating from his room. He beamed an evil older-brother grin at Sheldon and sized up The Brain.

"Whoa, *dude!*" said Sean, his eyes widening exaggeratedly. "Specky! Nice bins, bro!" He pointed at The Brain's glasses like he'd never seen anything so funny before in his life. Not for the first time, Sheldon wondered if Sean was adopted. He couldn't possibly come from the same gene pool as himself, could he?

"Hur, hur, hur! Glasses!"

The Brain made no acknowledgment of Sean's existence although Sheldon saw him glance at Sean's hand, which had a raw scrape running down it, ending at his wrist. A surfing wound, figured Sheldon.

"Have you finished, Sean?" said Sheldon, knowing full well he hadn't. From painful past experience he knew that Sean was probably just warming up.

"No, *loser,* I haven't finished. Mum said you had a friend up here, *loser,* and I just had to come up and see what he looked like...being so rare and all. He might even be the first one, right? And I tell you something, *loser,* this one was worth seeing!"

Sheldon sighed, the insults bouncing off him like

peas off a building. Years of brotherly verbal abuse had hardened his skin to the texture of a particularly tough rhino wearing a double-thickness elephant-skin coat. Sean threw a few more insults through the door before losing interest. After one last look at The Brain and a pitying shake of his surfing haircut, Sean lolloped back to his room, laughing all the way. There was a final blast of music before Sean closed the door. Yes, Sean had been a real tower of strength after Dad died, reflected Sheldon. Being charitable, Sheldon supposed that Sean had decided he needed to work out his grief by being as nasty to Sheldon as possible. Different strokes, and all that.

The Brain did not appear to have noticed Sean at all, but he did get his notebook out and write something down. Something about the way he did it made Sheldon hope there was nothing in that little black notebook about himself.

"So, Sheldon," he continued, looking up from the page. "My proposition. What is your reaction?"

There was a pause while Sheldon did an impression of a goldfish.

"I observe you are speechless," said The Brain, pointing his pipe at Sheldon. "And who can blame you, old top? After all, it isn't every day that you get asked to be the confidant, the chronicler, the aide-de-camp of The Greatest Living Detective on Earth!"

"And that would be...?"

"*Myself*, of course. Theophilus Nero Hercule Sherlock Wimsey Father Brown Marlowe Spade Christie Edgar Allen Brain, at your service!"

He jumped down off the chair and began to wave his pipe about, reminding Sheldon of an animated elf.

"You may have noticed my slightly large cranium. My head, Sheldon, my head," said The Brain, seeing the look on Sheldon's face.

Sheldon murmured something polite about not having noticed anything, but The Brain waved it away as unimportant with an impatient shake of his hand.

"Yes, yes, never mind all that. The important fact is that inside this skull lies a brain of unthinkably huge possibilities and abilities! Pray make yourself comfortable and I will tell you how it came about. It all happened many years ago and far away, at the Van Schekling Institute for Cranio-Biological Research in Zurich to be precise…"

Chapter 5

*T*he snow—please put down that pie, Sheldon my good fellow, it is something of a distraction and very bad for your health—*the snow lay four feet deep around the library at the Institute that fateful night. My parents, Professor Brian Brain and Professor Bryony Brain, young, good-looking and, of course, superintelligent, were the star research scientists at the Institute—who could forget their amazing Food Doubling Machine, the astonishing Self-Replicating Rocket Fuel, or their revolutionary work on Deep Space Hypersonic Matter Transportation?*

The night was going to be an exciting one. It was to be the first public display of the amazing new Gamma Wave Intelligence Enhancement Device, better known as the Genius Machine, on which my parents had been toiling for many years, and for which there was a positive frenzy of expectation from the scientific world.

The demonstration of the machine was to be held in the Leipzig Library, the only room large enough to accommodate the huge number of high-ranking scientists, fat-cat businessmen, and journalists interested in seeing what would be nothing less than a revolution in human intelligence.

Behind the large curtain shielding the stage from the audience was Dr. Dirk Unsinn, the Director of the Institute. He looked very happy.

"The Genius Machine looks everything you promised it to be, yes, I think!" he said. "All that remains is to give this public demonstration and then, global praise, a fortune in royalties for the Institute, the Nobel Prize. Of this I am certain, yes! You are ready for the press, Herr Professor?"

My father was too busy tinkering with the Genius Machine to hear Unsinn's prattle below, but my mother replied, "One moment, Dr. Unsinn. I will give you the signal."

Unsinn nodded to her and strode off to make the introductions.

The Genius Machine sat on a temporary stage at the end of the library, surrounded by towering mahogany shelves and under a massive crystal chandelier which cast a golden glow over the proceedings. In the main body of the room sat row after row of journalists and respected members of the scientific community. An expectant chatter filled the air.

My mother glanced anxiously toward my father, who nodded from his place on the ladder propped against the Genius Machine. It was ready! My mother placed me at the side of the stage, bent down, and kissed me on the top of my head.

"Wish me luck!" she said.

I remember those words precisely, Sheldon, for they were the last words she would ever speak to me.

Out on stage my mother tapped the microphone and began to speak.

"Good evening, esteemed colleagues, gentlemen and ladies of the press, Herr Direktor. Thank you all for coming out on this cold night to witness the first public demonstration of our little Genius Machine. A machine which, we believe, will increase the brain capacity of every man, woman, and child on the planet by a phenomenal amount. With no side effects noted in our extensive research, and extremely low building costs, our machine represents nothing less than a revolution in human science!"

There was a murmur from the audience and a few cameras flashed. My mother had their full attention.

"Think of the possibilities!" she continued. "No more stupid people! The end of radio phone-in shows! People in Florida would be able to count votes properly! Wrestling as a sport would die out completely! Above all, the world will become logical, precise, rational. All will be cool reasoning…"

As my mother talked, I began to lose interest. I was, after all, only four years old, and my main field of interest lay in Theoretical Mathematics and Interplanetary Rotational Gravity Flux Calculus.

Bored, I decided to explore the back of the Genius Machine to see if I could find my father. I could see his legs still hanging out of the top of the machine as he worked on a last-minute refinement. The silver sides of the Genius Machine stretched up amid a tangle of wires, scaffolding, and pipe-work. I began to haul myself up the scaffolding. After a minute or two I neared the top of the machine and looked down.

It was to prove a fatal error.

How I regret that moment, Sheldon! How things might have gone, had I not taken that glance!

But take it I did and, in looking down, my balance went. My head swam as I contemplated the dizzy height I had reached. Far below, my mother was talking. I clung to the scaffolding and hoped I would regain my composure. It was not to be.

"Look!"

A voice rang out from the audience below.

"A kid! Up there! He's gonna fall!"

Every face turned my way. My mother screamed.

"Theophilus!"

My father, alerted by the commotion, reacted quickly. He clambered swiftly through the tangle of equipment and reached a hand toward me. By now, balanced on the very lip of the machine, I was close to childish tears.

"Take my hand, Theo," urged my father. 'Take it, please!"

I wanted to reach forward but my fear got the better of me and instead I reached for a nearby cable.

"NOOOOO!" my father cried as the cable gave way under my weight.

I tottered on the brink for a moment, before falling directly into the Genius Machine. The cable I had taken hold of, and still clung to as I fell, was secured to the section of the library that contained the work of every known detective writer. The volumes tumbled down after me into the device in a paper avalanche, knocking my father to the stage below.

Sparks erupted from cracked electrical units as I pinballed down into the bowels of the machine. I could hear muffled screams of panic as the device heaved and groaned. The pressure inside was building fast; steam whistled viciously from broken pipes and a fearful, high-pitched whine was increasing by the second. What I feared most was hydrochloric acid leaking into the machine's central radioactive core and triggering an explo—

The sound was simply astonishing when it came.

A blinding crack of white light filled my senses and that was all I remember until I awoke in St. Ignatius Children's Hospital. They had all perished, Sheldon; all of them. Dr. Unsinn. The journalists. The cream of the scientific world. My parents. All gone in a single explosion. And all of it my fault. Mine alone.

The Brain paused and rubbed his eyes. Sheldon didn't know what to say. What *was* there to say? "Never mind?" "Oops?" How about, "Hey, I lost my dad, too, in a weird boating accident that no one can explain!" Before Sheldon could think of anything suitable, The Brain carried on with his story.

"Months, years even, of painful therapy followed. I would be lying to you, Sheldon, if I said it was not difficult; it was, even for me. As the swelling of my brain increased, I underwent operation after operation. I knew the surgeons by their first names. The medics thought my brain was swelling as a result of the explosion. They were right, it *was* getting bigger, my brain was growing rapidly...much quicker than should have been physically possible. Yet there it was. The evidence was there for all to see: the Genius Machine had worked!

"From that point I could not stop absorbing information. Already a bright child, as one would expect of the offspring of two brilliant scientific minds, my progress took wings! I devoured book after book, conducted experiments, learned languages, took knowledge from all cultures, all places. My mind fizzed with energy and excitement and I required little or no sleep.

"There was one peculiarity that stood out during this period, and that was my interest in crime and detection. It was only when I studied the police case file on the incident at the Institute that I realized what had happened. Remember the stack of books that fell into the machine with me? Somehow the device had taken all the information from all those detective stories and hardwired them directly into my supercharged brain.

"Months turned into years and my physical wounds gradually healed." The Brain replaced his pipe and gave it a thoughtful suck. "The authorities at St. Ignatius eventually traced my only remaining relatives to Farrago Bay, and here I am."

After an epic tale like that, Sheldon felt he had to say something.

"Erm..."

It was the best he could come up with on short notice.

Three things about The Brain's story were immediately obvious to Sheldon.

First, he was a total fruitcake—Genius Machine, my left nostril!

Second, he was a total fruitcake.

Third, and most worryingly of all, *he was a total fruitcake.*

Sheldon looked nervously at the bedroom door and rapidly calculated the distance to see if he could make it out before things turned nasty.

He had once seen a TV show where a bloke was trapped in a lift with a knife-wielding dipstick who thought he was the president of the United States. The bloke only managed to survive by pretending the dipstick actually *was* the Prez. While it was true that The Brain didn't have a knife and didn't think he was the president and Sheldon wasn't trapped in a lift with him, Sheldon still felt that his best chance of survival was to humor him. Sheldon pasted a look of total sincerity on his face and tried to pretend he believed The Brain's fairy tale.

"So, um, what does this business actually involve?" asked Sheldon.

"Oh, you know, being alongside me while I investigate mysteries. Writing down my exploits for the public interest and for scientists who may want to study my work some time in the future. You would also be responsible for saying things like: 'But what I don't understand is...'"

He paused.

"Every great detective has his trusted idio—, er, trusted *ally,* who stands shoulder to shoulder as they face criminal masterminds. Holmes had Watson, Poirot his Hastings. I shall have a *Sheldon!*"

He was so animated, so alive, so *persuasive,* that Sheldon found his initial distrust wavering. He still thought The Brain might be three spanners short of a full toolbox, but as he looked at him standing there something dawned on Sheldon.

What, after all, did he have to lose?

It wasn't like there was a stampede of kids at his door every night pleading with him to go play ball or swim or anything, was there? And as much as Sheldon loved his computer he couldn't depend on it for company the rest of his life. At the very least, The Brain was going to provide some fun one way or another. And he'd been spot on about all that quarry stuff with Snook downstairs, hadn't he? Maybe there was something in this after all. He might *even* have been telling the truth about the Genius Machine. *Something* must have caused him to get so weird, mustn't it? Besides, wasn't an entertaining fruitcake exactly what Sheldon needed right now?

Sheldon sat down on the edge of his bed and leaned forward.

"This sidekick thing. Does it pay?"

That evening The Brain talked into the night...well, until bedtime, anyway. He talked about the great fictional detectives, his skinny arms whirling and eyes gleaming as he spoke about Sherlock Holmes and Nero Wolfe, about Hercule Poirot and Miss Marple, Lord Peter Wimsey, Sam Spade, and Philip Marlowe. He talked about parsnips sinking into butter, about little gray cells, locked-room mysteries, and about it always being someone you wouldn't suspect, and Sheldon understood almost none of it. But as The Brain spoke, Sheldon had to confess he was hooked. Life at Farrago Bay wasn't all *that* exciting. Sheldon was starting to look forward to being The Brain's sidekick on all his big cases—

"Wait a minute," said Sheldon, suddenly thinking of a possible flaw in The Brain's grand scheme. "It's all very well talking about solving cases and doing all this detecting. But we're in Farrago Bay! Nothing exciting ever happens here!"

He meant of course that nothing exciting had happened since *The Coreal* disaster. That had seemed to use up Farrago Bay's supply of excitement for quite some time.

The Brain smiled and placed his pipe back between his teeth.

"Do you not read the local newspaper, Sheldon?" he said.

Sheldon shook his head. "I've been up here all day. I hadn't even spoken to Mum or Sean until you arrived."

"Then you haven't heard?"

"Heard what?"

"This," said The Brain. From his backpack he pulled a copy of the local newspaper, the *Farrago Bay Bugle,* flattened it out, and held it up in front of Sheldon.

Sheldon read. An advert in the small ads section had been circled in red.

For Sale: large quantity of lorikeet manure. Call Dr. Carefree O'Toole 6667 34333. Pet Psychiatry and bongo playing also available.

Sheldon looked at The Brain. "I don't get it. That's the big news?"

The Brain glanced at the newspaper and shook his head.

"My apologies, Sheldon. That is merely another matter which may be of some interest to our case. What I want you to look at is *this.*"

He rearranged the newspaper to show the front page and held it up once more.

BIFF MANLY TRAGEDY! BODY FOUND! screamed the headline in big black letters. Underneath was a picture of a police crime scene with some policemen standing outside a white tent. Snook was one of them.

There was a caption below the photo.

"Local police cordon off Henderson's Quarry after a body, believed to be that of local star surfer Biff Manly, was found floating in a slurry pit. Manly, star of the last three years State Surf Championships and holder of the world number twenty-eight spot, had been missing since Tuesday morning, thought drowned after a practice session off Perkins Point. Sergeant Snook of Farrago Bay Police refused to confirm rumors that they were still looking for Manly's left leg."

Biff Manly *dead*!

If The Brain had told Sheldon that David Beckham was going to be the new sports teacher at Farrago Bay High School, he'd have been less stunned. Biff was the most famous person the Bay had ever produced. Anyone who'd been brought up there knew all about Biff. Sheldon was used to seeing him walking around town, all blond and perfect, teeth and muscles, carrying his surfboard down to the beach. He was the local kid made good. The whole town had been buzzing when he'd picked up a big sponsorship deal earlier in the year with Dent-O Toothpaste: Sheldon recalled seeing a photo of him getting a check from some big cheese up at the new Dent-O factory after winning an important local competition. Biff and Sheldon's brother Sean had been up against one another in the surf-off before Biff got the decision after an "incident" out on the waves.

Biff now drove a shiny new curve-backed purple SUV and spent his life surfing in exotic locations around the world. Sean worked (sometimes) as a gofer for a local roofer.

Easy to work out who got the best deal.

Sheldon hadn't even known that the Farrago Surf God was missing but, then again, why should he? His world and Biff's were miles apart. Sheldon had only ever spoken to him once after accidentally hitting Biff's surfboard with his skull while Biff was riding in to shore. Sheldon hadn't been surfing, just flopping around in the shallows with the little kids and the pale tourists.

Sheldon had said something like "Urk! Agh! Gurgle!"

while Biff Manly's words—Sheldon could remember them clearly enough, even though he was busy swallowing eighteen liters of salt water and a spiny-backed whiting—were "McGlone, you *beepin'* little dweeb, you're as useless as that ugly loser brother of yours! You mighta scuffed me board!"

And now the Biffster was no more. Missing a leg too. Funny how things turn out sometimes, isn't it?

Something else occurred to Sheldon.

"Hey! All that detective stuff downstairs about Snook was made up! You knew he'd been to Henderson's Quarry all along *and* that he was a police sergeant!"

The Brain waved his pipe airily. "A trifling detail, Sheldon. I would have deduced all in exactly the same way even without the newspaper. I simply couldn't resist teasing Snook."

Sheldon nodded, although he was far from convinced. It still felt like cheating. He made a mental note not to be so impressed the next time The Brain did some "detecting."

"You must clear your mind of all that nonsense, dear boy," continued The Brain. "*This* is the challenge in front of us," he said, holding up the front page of the newspaper again. "We must solve The Mystery of the Missing Leg!"

Sheldon sat up. Brilliant! They would solve the Biff Manly case, catch his killer (although personally Sheldon still hadn't forgiven Biff for that smack on the head), and be the toast of Farrago—hooray! There might even be a reward from Dent-O.

"That's great!" said Sheldon. "But where do we start? How on earth are we going to solve this on our own? We don't have any, er, laboratories, or dogs, or anything—not even a car. Not many great detectives have to take the bus to the crime scene. We've got nothing, absolutely nothing to go on!"

"Well," said The Brain. "There is *one* thing we have to start with."

"Which is?"

"His leg, dear boy," said The Brain. "I found Biff Manly's leg."

Chapter 6

This was going to need a bit of explaining. "This is going to need a bit of explaining," Sheldon said. "You *found* his leg? What, was it just lying in the street somewhere and you tripped over it?"

"Not exactly, old thing. I did have—this."

The Brain bent down and pulled a small object from his backpack. It looked a little bit like a handheld computer game, which was funny because that's exactly what it was. Sheldon looked at The Brain and raised his eyebrows.

"You found Biff's leg with the aid of a Game Box?"

"Game Box *Advance,* Sheldon," said The Brain sternly.

"Oh well, Game Box *Advance.* How silly of me. That explains everything."

"Sarcasm is the last refuge of a bounder, Sheldon, didn't your mother teach you that? Now, pay attention. This Game Box Advance is no ordinary Game Box Advance. It has been modified a little. See?"

He held up the device. A small circuit board had been taped roughly to one side. Some orange and green wiring snaked around the back of the Game Box and disappeared into the innards.

"The simple addition of a few circuits turns this toy into a Global Positioning DNA Tracker—one of my own inventions—which can track genetic material anywhere on the planet. It's quite simple, really. I managed—don't ask how, the explanation is far too complex—to obtain a sample of Mr. Manly's DNA, fed it into the Global Positioning DNA Tracker, and, bishbosh, here we are."

The Brain pressed a button on top of the Game Box/Global Positioning DNA Tracker, and the screen flashed into electric green life.

"That's Mr. Manly's leg," said The Brain, pointing to a lighter-colored dot flickering in the center of the screen.

"Where is it?"

"In my quarters," said The Brain. "My bedroom," he added, seeing Sheldon's face. "But that's not where I found it..."

The Brain had found Biff Manly's left leg floating in a brackish pool in Coldcut Creek. There was nothing immediately noticeable about it, apart from the fact it was no longer connected to the rest of Biff Manly. However, on closer inspection there *were* one or two very interesting things about the leg that The Brain *did* think worthy of recording in his ever-present black notebook.

That it belonged to Biff was blindingly obvious. Blindingly obvious to The Brain, that is. The main clue was the black-and-red tattoo running down the back of the calf. The tattoo had the name "Farrago Flamers" underneath a snake riding a surfboard. The rest of the leg was typical of a seventeen-year-old surfer—sinewy, tanned, and marked by small cuts and grazes of varying age.

After his initial once-over, The Brain made a more thorough, detailed examination. Producing a powerful magnifying glass, he examined Manly's foot, noting hardened patches of skin along the outer edge. The Brain deduced that Biff Manly had been slightly pigeon-toed but that this was unlikely to be relevant. However, as any great detective knows, all facts, no matter how small, must be considered. Facts, The Brain knew, were the separate pieces of the jigsaw that, when assembled correctly, showed the picture in its entirety. The fact that a piece of the puzzle was merely a component was unimportant.

The first thing The Brain did was to make a drawing of the leg in his notebook. Fighting back repulsion at the decaying flesh in front of him, The Brain reminded himself of Sherlock Holmes's advice: a true student of the noble art would flinch at nothing—nothing at all—in order to achieve the result he desired.

By breathing only through his mouth, The Brain found he could reduce the stench to a manageable level. With a pen he gently lifted a great flap of skin to reveal Manly's femur gleaming ghost white in the gathering gloom. It had been snapped clean in two.

The Brain let the skin fall back into place, the slight motion causing the leg to bob gently in the water. He let out a long breath and took a moment to recover his composure. Squatting at the water's edge, The Brain watched the spreading ripples wobbling slightly as they passed over a log just below the surface. The leg itself rested against the muddy bank of the ditch, in a patch of ragweed and discarded candy wrappers, in precisely the position The Brain had found it ten minutes previously.

Now that he actually *had* the leg in his possession he needed to think about just what to do with it. The obvious thing, the thing most normal people would do, would be to call the police and tell them all about the leg.

However, The Brain was very far from being *normal*. For reasons of his own, he had no intention of handing the leg to Sergeant Snook or any other local investigator.

Instead, The Brain sat on the bank and thought about the awesome force that would have been needed to snap cleanly through Manly's thigh bone. He looked around the darkened clearing, his gigantic brain sifting furiously through the information at his disposal. In a few seconds he had come up with the answer. It was improbable, impossible even, but The Brain was in no doubt at all that there was one thing, and one thing only, that could have been responsible for the major injury to Manly's leg. It had to have been an animal. A large one. One with jaws capable of biting through the largest bone in the human body as if it were a toothpick.

In short, The Brain decided, he was looking for a crocodile.

Two seconds later he found one.

The surface of the creek erupted as an enormous, glittering, prehistoric nightmare of power and fury lunged at The Brain, its gaping jaws and gleaming teeth snapping at his ankle as he scrambled madly up the bank. If The Brain had not already computed the possibility that a crocodile was involved a split second before the ferocious onslaught, the reptile would surely have had him.

This crocodile was five meters long from blunt snout to sharp tail, and over nine hundred kilos; a heavyweight killing-machine sixty-five million years in the making. The Brain, his photographic memory rapidly recalling data from Briggs's REPTILES OF THE WORLD, estimated its weight to be 902 kilos soaking wet, its Latin name *Crocodilius omnivorium*. The information was interesting, but discarded as being of no immediate relevance. The Brain searched his internal data banks further for something useful. Immediately his memory began spitting out facts like machine-gun bullets.

Bang! Saltwater crocodiles are one of the fiercest creatures on the planet.

Bang! Saltwater crocodiles inhabit river areas in Northern Queensland, the Northern Territory, and northern Western Australia.

Bang! Saltwater crocodiles often grow as long as six meters in length.

Bang! Saltwater crocodiles are fiercely territorial.

Bang! Saltwater crocodiles lay about twenty-five eggs in a clutch.

Bang! Saltwater crocodiles often chase their prey for up to fifty meters in a straight line.

That was it!

Straight line. Crocodiles ran fastest in a *straight* line.

The Brain switched to running zigzag along the riverbank, his heart banging and legs weak from the powerful surge of adrenaline rushing through his body.

Over the next twenty meters a gap opened up between The Brain and the crocodile as it attempted to track his erratic movements. The crocodile was tiring, or perhaps growing bored. The Brain relaxed a little and risked a look over his shoulder.

As he did, he slipped, his foot jarring wickedly against an exposed root. The Brain slithered helplessly down the greasy mud bank toward the river before splashing to a stop on his back in seven centimeters of muddy water, dazed and breathless. He cursed his own stupidity and looked up as a shadow fell across him.

It was the crocodile. Now that The Brain had fallen, the crocodile had slowed. It was as if she knew his situation was hopeless. The Brain had nowhere to run, the river at his back, the crocodile in front. Time stood still. Even the mosquitoes appeared to freeze in midair. The only sound The Brain could hear was the rasp of his own breath and a deep, frightening rumble from the crocodile above him.

The Brain needed only one billion-billionth of his awesome intellect to confirm that he was to be the saltwater crocodile's next meal unless he could come up with something very quickly. With blistering hyper-sonic speed, his brain computed everything. The answer that came back at the speed of light was depressing: he was crocodile food.

The Brain closed his eyes and hoped that it wouldn't be too painful. The knowledge that crocodiles did not eat their victims straightaway, preferring to drown them and eat them later, did not make him feel any more comfortable. He waited, wet and trembling, for the first awful contact, the stink of the crocodile's rotten-meat breath hot against his face. Seconds ticked past. Then, instead of the expected bite, The Brain heard an odd hacking sound. He opened one eye and risked a peek.

It was incredible. Instead of attacking, the crocodile was moving her tail from side to side. It made the strange hacking sound once more.

The Brain adjusted his glasses.

He couldn't believe what he was seeing. Unless he was very much mistaken (and *that* did not happen very often), this particular example of *Crocodilius omnivorium* was...*barking*.

As in *barking* barking. Like a dog.

It was, The Brain had to admit, the strangest sight he had ever seen. Apart from the fact that dogs don't usually possess a two-meter-long tail and a row of extremely white teeth that could disembowel an antelope in less than six seconds, it was, he believed, unique to hear a crocodile barking.

The croc woofed once more and wagged her tail happily. Her meaning was clear: she wanted to play.

Slowly, experimentally, and feeling ever so slightly

silly, The Brain stood, picked up a large stick, and with a grunt threw it off to one side. In a flash, the crocodile chased after it, daintily picked it up in her mighty jaws, and ran back to The Brain. The croc dropped the stick, wagged her tail, and barked expectantly. The Brain threw it again and back it came once more.

"Singular," murmured The Brain. "Really most, most singular."

He looked around, half expecting a TV crew to step out from behind a tree with the news that this was all a setup involving a trained crocodile. But nothing like that happened. The crocodile rolled over onto its back and rolled its eyes at The Brain. The Brain hesitated (well you would, wouldn't you?) before bending down to tickle its belly. The crocodile squirmed with pleasure before rolling back onto its legs and barking again.

The Brain scratched his head. This was going to take some serious thought.

Sheldon listened open-mouthed to the story. The sounds of Sheldon's mother saying goodnight to Sergeant Snook drifted upstairs.

"The croc," said Sheldon. "What happened with the crocodile?"

The Brain opened his mouth.

"Sheldon! That's enough yakking for one night! Time for bed!" he said in a voice very like Mrs. McGlone's. It took Sheldon a second to realize that it *was* his mother yelling up the stairs.

"I shall reveal all tomorrow, old top," said The Brain, rising to his feet. "It is perhaps getting rather late. Besides, I have some observations I need to make at the supermarket."

"The supermarket? It'll be closed."

"Precisely, dear boy," said The Brain mysteriously. "I'm hoping that a little theory of mine will be confirmed."

Sheldon was about to speak when a bloodcurdling howl cut through the evening.

"SHEL-*DON!*"

Sheldon sighed. His mother had moved to DefCon 4. It was serious.

The Brain hopped down from the chair and hoisted his backpack onto his shoulder.

"Perhaps you could pop round after school tomorrow, Sheldon? Take a spot of tea while I explain."

Explanations would be nice. There were still a thousand unanswered questions about the Biff-Manly's-leg stuff. Not to mention The Brain's odd comment about the supermarket.

"But, but..."

The Brain held up his hand.

"Tomorrow will do, Sheldon, my good fellow. The leg will keep. In a manner of speaking." The Brain paused dramatically. "There is one final thought I will leave you to ponder this evening, old top. What was a prime specimen of saltwater crocodile doing fifteen hundred kilometers south of its usual habitat?"

And with that he was gone.

Chapter 7

Biff Manly, or what was left of him, lay on the steel gurney in the mortuary at Farrago Bay hospital. Sergeant Snook, along with a rather green-looking police constable, stood to one side as Annie Madison, the Farrago Bay coroner, finished her examination of the body. It was the part of his job that Snook had always hated, although this was only the second murder investigation he'd ever been part of. The few times previously he'd needed to be in the mortuary had involved drowned tourists or car crash victims. Those times were horrible enough, but there was something about this being murder that made it worse.

"So what have we got, Annie?" said Snook, trying very hard to sound like he attended murder autopsies on a daily basis.

"Well, he's definitely dead," said Annie Madison. "I'm one hundred percent sure on that point. From there on in, it's all a bit of a puzzle, even for someone as clever as me."

Snook's shoulders sagged. "I had been hoping for

something to go on, Annie. You know, a clue or something."

"Well, I did find a blood-spattered note with the murderer's name written on it clutched in Biff's hand," she said as she washed her own hands in the large metal sink.

Snook quivered. "Really? That's great! Who was it?"

Annie gave him a scornful look.

"Of course I didn't, you idiotic flatfoot! That only happens in books. No, this one *is* a puzzler. Look."

She bent over Biff once more. Reluctantly Snook moved closer. PC Higgins moved his head a centimeter nearer and held his handkerchief even tighter.

"Mr. Manly died from a head wound, most likely from a fall into Henderson's Quarry," said Annie. "But he had suffered quite a few injuries before that."

"The leg, you mean?" said Snook.

"No, his leg was still attached when he died. I mean all these little scratches and bites. They all happened while he was still alive."

"A fight? A disagreement over something? We *have* heard he'd argued with another surfer not long before he disappeared."

"Perhaps," said the coroner. "But it would have been a very strange fight. If you want my best guess, I'd say that Manly had a fight with someone or a group of people, was badly beaten, and then fell—perhaps while trying to escape—into Henderson's Quarry, which is where he got the head wound. His leg was removed at some point after his fall: there'd have been more blood if it had been taken off while he was alive—are you feeling all right, Constable? But all that's just guesswork. The two events, the fight and the head wound, happened at almost the same time."

She looked down at the place where Biff's leg had been removed.

"As for how the leg was taken, I really don't know what to suggest except to say that it was not pulled off, it didn't drop off, and it wasn't removed for surgical reasons. If I didn't know better, I'd say it had been bitten off."

Snook looked at her.

"Bitten off? By what? A shark?"

"Last time I looked there were no sharks in Henderson's Quarry, Sergeant. The quarry pond does lead into the creek, but it's far too shallow and narrow for sharks to travel that far upstream. And people would have noticed if Biff had been minus a leg before he disappeared, don't you think?"

Snook wrote some notes down.

"Not. A. Shark. Got that," he murmured.

Annie Madison rolled her eyes and pulled on her jacket.

"I need to get over to Balloona. Lawyer fell into a wood chipper."

"Blimey!" said Snook.

"Yes, very nasty, completely ruined a perfectly good wood chipper. I wish there was something more I could help you with," said Annie Madison. "But this one has got me stumped. Get it?"

She pulled a sheet over Biff's body, patted Snook on the shoulder, nodded to PC Higgins, and left. Snook put his notebook away and followed. He didn't want to stay in there for any longer than was necessary.

Six minutes after everyone had left, the steel door to the mortuary slid open silently. A white-coated blond man, who could have been a hospital technician but was not, slipped inside and approached the table. He pulled back the sheet and looked at the body without a flicker of emotion. It wasn't the first corpse he'd seen and he didn't expect it would be the last. From a pocket the man produced an envelope. Carefully, with a pair of tweezers, he pulled a few brown hairs from inside. He lifted Biff's hand and, with rubber-gloved fingers, inserted the hairs under Biff's fingernails. Satisfied, he put the envelope and tweezers back in his pocket, replaced the sheet and, after a final check around the room, padded out as silently as he'd arrived.

Chapter 8

After The Brain left, sleep had not come easy to Sheldon McGlone. Normally he dropped straight into an untroubled heavy-headed slumber with almost embarrassing ease, but tonight was different. He flipped and turned on his pillow like a sailor on a storm-tossed sea.

When sleep finally did arrive, patchy and unsatisfying, it had brought with it unpleasant dreams.

The dreams, like most dreams, came in fragments. Biff's leg was featured, together with a large crocodile wearing flowered underwear. At one point the croc was cleaning its teeth with a large toothbrush and playing Trivial Pursuit with The Brain while they were being chased by a gang of Keystone Cops in bright blue uniforms. The lead cop looked like Snook, except he also looked like Julia Roberts the movie actress.

"Who played the part of—" shouted the crocodile as they ran.

"Ping!" said The Brain, "Tommy Lee Jones. Keep running!"

"Hoy!" shouted Snook/Julia Roberts. "Stop!"

Then Sheldon's brother Sean arrived and turned everything black and white. Sheldon reached down and fiddled with the controls and found himself back in glorious living color.

Sheldon rather wished that at that point a wise old man would appear and give him a vital clue to solve the mystery, but all that happened was that a gang of armed blowfish started lip syncing to a popular rock song. Then things got *really* silly and Sheldon was glad to wake up in a slick of sweat back in his own bed.

After time spent in a pointless effort to drift off once more, Sheldon gave up and wobbled blearily across to his computer. Destined not to sleep, he could at least spend the time helping to solve The Mystery of the Missing Leg. That was what sidekicks did, right? Besides, the sun was almost up. He wondered if he should get dressed and go out to help The Brain somehow. But he didn't know if his arrival would spoil any of The Brain's theories. Besides, it might be dangerous out there. Sheldon decided he would be more useful staying home and getting some background information.

He clicked onto the internet and spent time finding out lots of interesting and worrying facts about saltwater crocs. Everything The Brain had told him was true. Crocodiles were *never* found this far south and, if The Brain was to be believed, here was one knocking around Farrago Bay, fifteen hundred kilometers outside normal crocodile territory. Food for thought.

Thinking of food—and tiring of crocodile facts—

Sheldon went downstairs for some well-earned breakfast. His mother and Sean were already there. His mother started work at eight and Sean had been out surfing.

Keen to discover exactly what The Brain had really done with Biff's leg, Sheldon ate his cereal in a hurry.

"Where's the fire, McGlone?" said his mother from somewhere inside the cloud of smoke that hovered around her head.

"Hrrrn?" Sheldon crunched through a double mouthful of cereal. "Whash sfire?"

"God!" said Sean. "Close yer trap while you're eating, dude! That's just like, *nasty.*"

Sheldon noticed that Sean had bandaged his scratched hand.

"You hear about Biff?" Sheldon said.

Sean nodded but said nothing.

"What do you think happened to him?" said Sheldon. "Do you think they'll find the killer?"

"What is all this? How do I know?" spat Sean. "Don't you have school to go to or something? Jeez!"

He got up suddenly from the table and stalked upstairs.

"What did I say?" Sheldon asked his mother.

She shrugged and continued rattling stuff around the kitchen. His mother seemed to do a lot of that.

Sheldon threw his bowl in the sink, pecked his mother on her cheek—at least he thought it was her cheek, the smoke made it hard to tell—and headed for the door. He paused on the doorstep, remembering something: his mother worked in the Schools

Admissions Office down at the council HQ. Maybe *she* knew something about The Brain and his amazing incident with the Genius Machine.

"Mum, do you know anything about that new English kid at school?"

"Your new friend? That kid who was round last night? The one with the funny manners and the big he—?"

Sheldon nodded.

"Well, I'm not supposed to tell anyone *anything* about the information that I see down at the AO," said Mrs. McGlone, taking another lungful of smog.

Sheldon knew full well that his mother had a gob that could fit the Harbor Bridge in sideways and still have room for pedestrians, though she imagined she was as tight-lipped as a super-glued safe.

"But I can make an exception for you," she said out of the side of her mouth, one eye squinting against the smoke. "One thing, though; you got it all wrong about where your new friend's from. That kid isn't English," she finished, taking a supersize drag on her ciggie. "He's from Mooloolaba."

"*Mooloolaba?*" Sheldon squeaked. "Mooloolaba?"

"What, is there an echo in here? Yes, Mooloolaba. Got transferred in when his parents moved down here, I heard. His dad works up at Dent-O, I think. His mother's a bit standoffish, doesn't say much. Met her at the IGA a few nights ago. Big lady. Nola, she's called, Nola Brain. Husband's called Don or something and, according to Millie Halligan, he's kind of quiet too. Handsome though, I heard. Mustache."

"But what about—"

Sheldon was about to ask her more but stopped. Suddenly he didn't want to know anything else. If what she said was true then it meant that pretty much everything The Brain had told him last night must have been a lie. There had been no Genius Machine, no Zurich Incident, no explosion. The Brain was just some kid from Mooloolaba with a big head and a hyperactive imagination.

And of course that probably meant he hadn't found Biff Manly's leg at all.

Sheldon's dreams of fame and fortune melted like so many vampires after sunrise. He slumped out of the door, his glorious career as chief sidekick to The World's Greatest Detective shot down in flames before it could even begin.

That day at school was frustrating. On the bus going in, Sheldon planned to icily ignore The Brain all day and make him suffer for telling all those great big fibs. Mooloolaba! However, as there was no sign whatsoever of The Brain at school, Sheldon had no chance to give him the cold shoulder. Nothing is more frustrating than really wanting to teach someone a lesson by ignoring them totally, only to find that the person isn't even there to ignore. Sheldon had to content himself with a long session of silent fuming but, as any fool knows, silent fuming is no substitute for icy ignoring.

The Brain didn't show for recess or lunch, either.

By two o'clock Sheldon began to wonder if he'd imagined the whole of the previous night's conversation, or possibly even the existence of someone called The Brain. Now that he thought about it, it didn't sound very likely: "The Brain."

Just before the last lesson of the day (Class 8C were studying the influence of hairspray on Shakespearean sonnets or something equally relevant), Sheldon found a note in his locker.

Weird.

The note hadn't been there at the end of lunchtime, and Sheldon didn't think anyone had been inside apart from Jakes, the school janitor, who didn't count.

However the note had arrived, Sheldon was pretty sure that no one from 8C had managed to slip the thing in his locker...but there it was, right in front of him.

Dear Sheldon,

Events overnight mean that I have been working undercover today and it was necessary for me to stay away from school. It is vital that you make your visit this evening no matter what you may have been told. Dark forces may be at work and I fear that your family may be in peril! Six PM. 54 Dibdob Drive.

Your friend, Theophilus

How had The Brain managed to get the note into Sheldon's locker? And what was all that about "no matter what you may have been told"? Who was in peril, and why? What dark forces? Questions buzzed around

Sheldon's head like a swarm of bees. Some of the questions stung too.

Before he could do much more thinking, Fleming sniffed loudly and, in a voice like a rusty public address system, barked out an order at him. "Sheldon McGlone! Report to the office immediately!"

"*Jawohl*," said Sheldon, careful to keep it under his breath.

He gathered his belongings and slipped out of the classroom, a farewell spitball from Fergus Feebly seeing him on his way.

As he approached the headmaster's office, Sheldon could see smoke wafting under the door. It was possible that the school was on fire, or a big rock band was using dry ice during a quick gig in the headmaster's office, but of all the possibilities Sheldon considered, it was most likely the smoke belonged to his mother.

It did.

"Oh, Sheldon!" she wailed from somewhere inside her cloud. "It's Sean! They *arrested* Sean!"

"Sean?" said Sheldon stupidly, still trying to deal with the sight of his mother clutching the headmaster's jacket and crying all down his best white shirt. She was taller than him by at least fifteen centimeters, so she had to stoop to get her head against his chest.

"What's happened to Sean?"

Mrs. McGlone wailed again before lighting another cigarette and taking a puff in one quick smooth motion. One-handed too.

"Er, I think I've already mentioned that there's no smoking on school property, Mrs. McGlone," said Mr.

Herschfield in a voice that was one level higher than a beetle's whisper. "It's a health matter. Also there's the fire risk."

Mr. Herschfield was right about the fire risk: the tip of Mrs. McGlone's cigarette was brushing against his suit in a very flammable way.

"Oh, come on, Phil, cut me some slack here!" shouted Sheldon's mother. "Can't you see this is an *emergency*?"

Phil? thought Sheldon. Since when did his mother call Mr. Herschfield "Phil?" Best not to ask. What you don't know can't hurt you. Herschfield caught Sheldon's eye and looked a little sheepish. Sheldon wondered if the sergeant knew his mum called Herschfield "Phil."

"Erm, Sean?" said Sheldon, getting back to the matter at hand. "What's happened with Sean, exactly?"

"I'm afraid I have some bad news, Sheldon," said "Phil." "Your brother's been arrested."

"For what? It can't be anything too serious. Sean doesn't have the imagination."

"Oh for god's sake, Sheldon!" said Mrs. McGlone. "He's been arrested for *murder*. Arrested for *Biff Manly's* murder!"

Well.

Sheldon had to admit he hadn't seen that one coming. Sean? *Murdering* Biff Manly?

Sheldon considered how likely it was and realized, with something of a jolt, that it was all *too* likely when you sat down and thought about it.

1)   Sean *had* lost out to Biff in the Scuzzball Surf-off.

2) Sean hated Biff. It was common knowledge.

3) Sean had a mysterious cut on his hand.

4) Sean had been out late on the very day the *Bugle* said that Manly had disappeared.

When Sheldon put it all together like that it did look pretty much like an open-and-shut case, but he decided to stay quiet about his conclusion. Whether Sean was guilty or not, Sheldon had an idea that his mother wouldn't take it too well if he started getting dibs on Sean's room before the ink was dry on the arrest sheet.

Chapter 9

When Sheldon and his mother arrived at Farrago Bay police station, Sean was eating pizza on the front steps.

Farrago Bay police station didn't look like a high-security joint but this seemed plain ridiculous to Sheldon. Wasn't Sean a murder suspect? Shouldn't they be taking things a bit more seriously, even if he *was* Sheldon's brother and this *was* Farrago Bay? Besides, Sheldon had been really looking forward to seeing Sean behind bars, if only for the novelty value.

"They let you go already!" said Mrs. McGlone, beaming.

Sean looked up, his mouth chewing rhythmically.

"Nah, one of me surf mates is on the desk and said I could get some grub as long as I was back by three," he said through a mouthful of pepperoni.

The doors to the station opened and a red-faced Snook emerged blinking into the midafternoon sun. Alongside him was a smooth-looking man in a smart suit carrying a briefcase. His eyes slid across Sheldon like ice across marble. He focused on Sean and pointed.

"Get this killer back behind bars where he belongs!" he snapped.

"Oh…er, righto," said Snook, stepping forward and taking hold of Sean's arm. Mrs. McGlone grabbed Snook and pointed at the man in the suit.

"Who's this bloke?"

"Er…," said Snook.

"I'm Howard Horrocks, Mrs. McGlone," said the man coldly, and Sheldon remembered where he'd seen him before. Howard Horrocks, the Big Cheese up at—

"I'm the Managing Director of Dent-O, Mrs. McGlone, the—"

"I don't care if you're the Grand Poo-Bah of Eastern China, you perfumed piranha! What's my son got to do with you?"

She glared at him, their noses almost touching.

"Dent-O was proud to sponsor Biff Manly," said Horrocks. "He was a shining example of Australian manhood, cruelly murdered at the peak of his powers by your son. It is my, and Dent-O's, wish that the full majesty of the law is used against Biff's killer!"

Horrocks paused and shot Snook a meaningful look.

"Ah," said Snook miserably. "There's another thing, Mary. Mr. Horrocks here says that he, um, that is…"

"I saw the whole thing. Saw with my own eyes what he did. Your son bashed Biff so hard that he killed him and then he dumped his body in Henderson's Quarry! God only knows what vile impulse was behind him taking Biff's leg off! Poor Biff was covered in scratches and bites. He must have put up a hell of a fight!"

"Sorry, Mary," said Snook. "But it doesn't look good for the boy. You heard Mr. Horrocks. He saw everything."

"I keep tellin' ya, I didn't flamin' well do anything!" yelled Sean. "I haven't talked to that cheatin' scumbucket in months!"

"C'mon, sonny," said Snook. "You're only making things worse for yourself."

Horrocks ducked backwards as Sean was pulled into the station. "Very disturbed boy you have there, Mrs. McGlone! Very disturbed." He grinned wolfishly. "Then again, from what I hear about your family, *that's* not exactly a surprise. Didn't your husband manage to lose some tourists a couple of years ago? Not to mention himself. Careless."

Sheldon's mother took a swing at Horrocks and would have caught him if Sheldon hadn't grabbed her from behind and hauled her back. Not that Sheldon would have minded Horrocks getting a punch in the nose, but he didn't want another member of the family behind bars. Mrs. McGlone said some words to Horrocks that Sheldon hadn't heard before. Not from his mother anyway.

Sean was still struggling at the door.

"Hey, dude," he said, pointing at Horrocks. "You didn't see a thing! You didn't see a thing because nothing happened!"

"Really?" said Horrocks. "Then how do you account for Biff's demise?"

"His murder," explained Sheldon seeing Sean's puzzled face. "He's talking about Biff's murder."

Sheldon thought of something. "If you saw every-thing," he said, looking at Horrocks, "then why did you wait until now to tell Snook all about it?"

Horrocks licked his lips, looking for a moment like a cornered snake. Snook frowned. Sheldon could see he'd struck a nerve.

"There's a perfectly rational explanation for that!" said Horrocks, whose brow was beginning to bead with sweat.

"You see?" said Snook. "There's a perfectly rational explanation!"

"Then what is it?" said Sheldon. "What's the per-fectly rational explanation?"

There was an awkward pause while Snook looked at Horrocks and Horrocks looked at Snook.

"Amnesia!" Horrocks blurted the word out. "That's why! I had amnesia...temporary amnesia brought on by the, um, by the...erm..."

"By the trauma of witnessing such a horrible crime," said Snook helpfully.

Sheldon rolled his eyes.

"Yes, yes, that's exactly what happened!" spluttered Horrocks. "Thank you, Sergeant Snook. I had amnesia brought on by seeing your nasty son murder Biff Manly! Horrible it was, horrible!"

Mrs. McGlone stepped closer to Horrocks. "Yeah, well, Mr. Dent-O, amnesia or no amnesia, we're gonna prove that Sean is innocent! We're gonna get the best lawyer money can buy!"

Horrocks smiled nastily.

"I've just met your lawyer, Mrs. McGlone," he said in a low voice. "Don't get your hopes up."

With that, he turned on his shiny heels and slithered away into a long, gleaming car, its door held open by a stern-looking blond man. He got in, the door slammed, and they drove off up Main Street.

A few minutes later everyone had crammed into a tiny interview room where Sean's lawyer was waiting.

"We had to appoint a lawyer, Mary," said Snook. "Even if he's only…"

"Only what?" said Mrs. McGlone. "Even if he's only what?"

Snook said nothing. He looked across at Sean's court-appointed lawyer. The lawyer looked about sixteen years old and had a full crop of angry pimples. He was dressed in a suit that might have been fashionable sometime around 1988. The good news was that he *was* actually a lawyer. They knew this because he proudly showed them his certificate. The bad news was that he'd qualified last week and this was his first case. Unless you included that big parking-fine job he'd been on last Tuesday.

"But gee whiz, don't worry, Mrs. McGlone," said the lawyer, whose name was Perelman. "I've been reading up on this stuff for *ages!*"

It was official: Sean had the Worst Lawyer in History.

Sean was still picking pizza out from between his teeth. Could it *really* be possible, wondered Sheldon again, that they shared the same DNA? Another thing occurred to Sheldon. If Sean was innocent (and even though there were times when Sheldon would have cheerfully murdered *Sean,* he was utterly convinced that Sean was incapable of murdering anyone), then that meant Horrocks was lying. There was all that stuff about amnesia for a start. Plus, Sheldon realized with a shock, if Sean had fought and killed Biff, why did Sean have so few marks on him? Horrocks had said that Biff was covered in bites and scratches. Sean did have a scratch on his hand, true, but Sheldon would have expected more if Sean had fought with Biff. Biff would have been no pushover. No, Horrocks was lying all right. The big question was why?

It was time to get some help.

Chapter 10

Sheldon," said The Brain, opening his bedroom door a crack and squinting out. "You are a trifle early, but no matter. Good of you to come over, old top. I'd like your opinion about, um, something."

Sheldon waited for the door to open fully, desperate to tell The Brain the news about Sean, but The Brain stayed where he was, looking through the opening, his face streaked with mud. In the background Sheldon could hear rap music on the stereo. He was doing a lot of swearing—the rapper, not The Brain.

Sheldon had been shown upstairs by a large woman, probably the Nola his mother had been talking about, who hadn't said a word or changed her expression since answering the door. She didn't ask Sheldon who he was, or why he was there, she just waved him upstairs and resumed her vigil in front of the television, which was tuned to a foreign-language news program. A man with hair shaved close to his skull sat stiffly on an armchair, as if unused to such luxury. His back was ramrod straight and he looked at Sheldon through glacial blue eyes. He too said nothing at all. Sheldon was busting to ask them about The Brain and Mooloolaba, but couldn't find the right words. Somehow it didn't seem right to simply blurt out, "Excuse me, Mr. and Mrs. Brain, but is your son the World's Greatest Detective, somehow arrived here from Zurich via England, or is he just Theo Brain, some kid from Mooloolaba with an overactive imagination?"

Instead, Sheldon had opted to say nothing, walked upstairs, and knocked on the bedroom door. Nothing happened, because he'd actually knocked on the bathroom door, but after a few moments of looking around he managed to locate the right one.

The Brain held up a hand, palm outwards.

"One moment, my good fellow. There is something I need to confirm before you enter: once inside this room I must ask you to remain calm *no matter what happens.* Is that clear?"

"If it's the leg," said Sheldon, "I think I'll be OK."

The Brain looked puzzled for a moment. "Um, yes, the leg. There is that to consider also. Now, do I have your word that you will not scream, or ever reveal what you might see inside this room?"

Sheldon wondered what The Brain had meant by "also." Wasn't the leg enough?

"Yeah, sure, whatever. How bad can it be?"

The Brain slowly opened his bedroom door and Sheldon walked in. The air was thick with the heavy smell of incense and something else, something that Sheldon couldn't quite identify.

The room was larger than Sheldon had expected.

Books lined the walls: thick reference books, leather-bound and old. Looking around, Sheldon figured it was a good bet that the shelves held just about every fact about everything in the universe. There was also row upon row of detective fiction, all in exact alphabetical order.

A sleek and extremely powerful-looking matte-black computer of a type Sheldon had never seen before sat humming gently on The Brain's desk, a stack of CDs by its side. On-screen, a graphic seemed to be following the progress of a large incoming file. The graphic was in Japanese. There was also a small window in the corner of the monitor showing a high-definition image of the outside of The Brain's house.

Above the desk, on a series of shelves, were a bewildering variety of objects. A large glass skull, polished to a sheen, peered down from a shelf where it competed for space with a professional-looking microscope, a detailed globe, a framed letter from the president of the United States thanking The Brain for his help (it looked genuine but can't have been, surely?), and a chessboard. The Brain told Sheldon he was playing e-mail chess with a grand master who lived in Reykjavik. From the look of the board, The Brain was winning. The chessboard was next to a plaster cast of a shoe print (a Post-it note attached read "check manufacturer's data") and a whole library of language tapes and books. A teach-yourself-Cantonese book was open on a bedside table next to six labeled clocks showing the time in New York, London, Tokyo, Sydney, Easter Island, and Vancouver.

A large corkboard on one wall was covered in news-paper clippings. Sheldon noticed several of them related to *The Coreal* disaster. Other clippings dealt with various animal stories. "Monkey Escapes from Island Laboratory," "Man Bitten by Chicken," "Local Resident Claims Snake Can Sing," "Hawks Attack Residents in Rio." A map, downloaded from a wildlife internet site, seemed to show koala movements around Farrago Bay, outlined with red pen. Another set of photographs showed the rear view of the local supermarket taken through a telephoto lens.

Against one wall was a large boom box. Above it, in neatly ordered racks, was a huge collection of rap and hip-hop music. A signed photo showed The Brain standing, unsmiling, between two world-famous rappers. Sheldon peered at it closely to see if it was a Photoshop fake. He squinted closely but the image revealed no visible flaws. It looked real enough, although Sheldon had to admit he was no expert.

Sheldon's head whirled with questions. Could it all have been genuine? If it was, how did a kid from Mooloolaba get letters from the president of the United States and photos of gangsta rappers? Did Sheldon's mother have all the facts right? Why is it so difficult to find the start of a roll of sticky tape?

Sheldon shook his head and tried to concentrate on the one thing, despite all the competition, that dominated the room: Biff Manly's left leg, which lay on a steel bench next to the bed. Technically, Sheldon supposed that he didn't *know* it was Biff's leg, but how many spare legs could there be floating around in a town the size of Farrago Bay?

"Oh, man!" said Sheldon, suddenly feeling very ill indeed.

The leg, resting on top of a gray garbage bag, was lit by a powerful lamp. A microscope stood on the desk alongside it, together with several impressive-looking magnifying lenses and a book on anatomy. Despite the various incense burners around the room there was a distinct stench—of leg, Sheldon imagined, although never having smelled a decaying leg before he couldn't be sure.

Sheldon tried to collect his thoughts.

"Jeez. I mean, whoa—oh man, oh boy, oh, um, like, um."

Obviously Sheldon's mouth wasn't going to cooperate so he pointed at the bench, his finger trembling.

"Man, you really *do* have it!" Sheldon yelped. After his mother's bombshell about The Brain and Mooloolaba, there had been more than a slight doubt The Brain had the leg at all. Yet here it was, large as life. In a manner of speaking.

"That's a *leg*, man. A real, honest-to-god *leg*! And it's...in your room!"

After a few moments Sheldon got himself under control and turned to The Brain, who was sitting calmly on the leather chair in front of the computer.

"Told you I wouldn't scream, though," Sheldon said, a smug grin on his face as he sat down on The Brain's bed.

There was a sudden rumble and Sheldon felt the bed shudder before it lifted clear of the floor with him perched on top. The ceiling suddenly got a lot closer.

This didn't feel good.

"Actually, old top," said The Brain. "The leg wasn't what I wanted to warn you about."

Sheldon peered over the edge of the bed and looked down.

Between his feet, an enormous, river-green, scaly snout poked out very slowly, followed by the rest of a five-meter long, one-hundred-percent genuine, saltwater crocodile.

One of the most dangerous animals on the planet.

And it was in The Brain's bedroom.

With Sheldon.

"Bow, wow, wow, yippy-oh, yippy-ay," sang the rapper on the CD.

Sheldon couldn't agree with him more. Bow wow *wow.*

In no time, The Brain's room seemed to have filled up almost completely with crocodile. Small items of furniture in the room cracked and fell as the reptile uncoiled itself and stretched lazily. A stink of river mud and weed oozed out from under the bed and hung in the air, thick as jelly, completely overpowering the smell from the leg (the *leg*! What with a monster crocodile emerging unexpectedly from under the bed, Sheldon had almost forgotten about Biff's leg!). The bed dropped back, slanted now against the wall, and Sheldon found his legs poking toward the ceiling.

The Brain seemed very cool about it all.

Sheldon, on the other hand, was beginning to have serious doubts about the whole sidekick business. All thoughts of asking The Brain to help get Sean out of jail had been temporarily forgotten with the arrival of a crocodile on the scene. This hadn't been part of the deal.

The crocodile stopped moving and inspected Sheldon over the edge of the upturned bed, its snout just centimeters from his face. Sheldon couldn't help but notice how incredibly white and sharp the crocodile's teeth were. It was so close he could feel its stinking dinosaur breath on his skin and Sheldon wondered if that would be the last thing he'd remember. Apart from the biting, of course. Sheldon was trying very hard not to think about the getting-eaten part.

Sheldon's tongue was dry, his throat a desert. His heart did its best to escape through his nose and Sheldon didn't even want to *think* what might be happening in his bottom area.

There was, Sheldon considered, only one sensible response to being trapped in a bedroom with a large carnivorous reptile. He sucked in a big breath in order to scream as loudly as possible for as long as possible.

As the air rushed across Sheldon's vocal cords, The Brain jammed his hand over Sheldon's mouth, almost popping Sheldon's eyeballs out of his head with back-blow pressure.

"I'm fairly sure it won't harm you, old top," The Brain murmured in Sheldon's ear. "Understand? This creature thinks it's a *dog*. Now, if I take my hand away will you promise on your honor not to scream?"

Sheldon nodded, keeping his eyes firmly fixed on the crocodile. He was still fairly keen on the screaming option but for some reason didn't use it. Did that mean he trusted The Brain? Later, after the whole thing was over, Sheldon realized that the moment he met the crocodile was the moment he knew *for certain* that The Brain was most definitely For Real, whether he was from Mooloolaba or not.

The Brain removed his hand from Sheldon's mouth.

"That, that, that, that, that, that, that, that, that, that, that, that, that, that, that, that…"

The Brain helpfully jogged his arm and Sheldon managed to finish the sentence.

"That's a *crocodile*, Brain! A bogging croc! In your bogging bedroom!"

"Your powers of observation are, as usual, completely accurate, my dear Sheldon. You correctly identified the leg earlier as a leg, and now you are keeping your average up by postulating that the animal you see before you is a crocodile. I am pleased to say that you are correct; this is indeed a crocodile. In fact, she is a prime adult example of *Crocodilius omnivorium,* or saltwater crocodile. I call her Mavis."

A short while later, after a couple of calming choc bars from The Brain's secret stash of top-quality British confectionery, Sheldon's nerves had been de-jangled enough for him to sit on the slanting bed. The Brain had been sure to give Mavis her share of chocolate first; the croc was addicted to sweets of any kind, he explained. He'd been using them to help control her.

"It's not good for her teeth but, frankly, that's not of paramount importance right now…although Mavis's dental condition may be of some significance if my theories are correct."

Sheldon couldn't imagine how Mavis's teeth could

be important but he said nothing. He hadn't been a sidekick long but he was already gaining a healthy respect for The Brain's detecting powers.

Right now the Great Detective was absentmindedly tickling Mavis on her pale underbelly as she lay upside down on the floor. Sheldon didn't feel ready to get quite that cozy with the croc, but at least now he was fairly sure he had full control of his rear end. When Mavis had first appeared out from under The Brain's bed, it was touch and go whether he might have (how can this be put politely?) pooped his pants.

And who could have blamed him if he had? It's not every day you find yourself sharing room space with a five-meter killer crocodile with an identity crisis. Anyway, Sheldon *didn't* poop, which was something, he supposed. The Brain, for one, was probably glad—Sheldon didn't think Mavis would have noticed.

On the stereo, the rap music had changed to a softer, jazzier beat, which Mavis seemed to prefer. She bobbed her massive head in time, happily munching on marshmallows, which The Brain slipped into her mouth now and again.

"I have been trying to find some clues as to why this crocodile is behaving in such a way," he said. "And, if I am honest, I have been completely unable to track down a single example of a crocodile wishing to become a dog. I did find a few cases where cats or ducks had been raised by dogs, but nothing even close to this."

"Perhaps she, I mean Mavis, is tired of being a crocodile," suggested Sheldon. "Maybe being a dog looks like more fun?"

Mavis lifted her back leg and tried to scratch behind her ear in a doggy fashion. Sheldon wasn't even sure if crocodiles *had* ears. Bits of The Brain's stuff dropped off a shelf. He didn't appear to notice.

"Hmm," said The Brain, considering the question of Mavis's behavior. "It's true that crocodiles *are* very adaptable. In the deserts of West Africa there are crocodiles who tunnel ten meters beneath the sand to survive the dry season, but I don't think that's what Mavis is doing: adapting, I mean. No, I think this may have something to do with the leg, Sheldon. There is something very odd about that leg that I have not been able to..."

He trailed off, lost in thought for a moment, out there in the strange land where only brainy people go. Then he was back.

The Brain bent over Biff's leg, the smell of which was now getting more than a little funky, if Sheldon was being honest. In fact, if you mixed in the thick riverbed stench of Mavis, and The Brain's fine collection of old socks scattered around the room, the whole place was becoming stinky enough to bring tears to the eyes of a skunk.

"Look at this," said The Brain. Sheldon leaned about three millimeters in the direction of the leg, his hand over his mouth.

"No, Sheldon, old top, you *really* need to look at this."

Reluctantly Sheldon lowered his head toward the magnifying glass which The Brain held above the messy end of Biff's leg. He looked at the torn edges of skin and felt himself getting dizzy. Through a buzzing in his head, Sheldon heard The Brain say something.

"What?" said Sheldon. "What did you say?"

"The teeth marks. Look at the teeth marks, Sheldon. Observe how small they are."

"Um—of course, the teeth marks. Yes."

Sheldon forced himself to look and, to his surprise, he saw that The Brain was right. The leg was covered in small bite marks. In spite of feeling dizzy, Sheldon started to get interested. The bite marks also reminded him why he'd come over to The Brainhouse in the first place.

"Horrocks said Biff's body was covered in bites and scratches!" said Sheldon.

"Who is Horrocks?" said The Brain. "And how does he know Biff's body was covered in bites and scratches?"

Sheldon quickly filled The Brain in on everything that had happened since Sean's arrest. The Brain produced his notebook and scribbled inside.

"All the details, dear boy, I need all the details! Omit nothing!" said The Brain. He was particularly interested in Horrocks, the managing director at Dent-O, being the only witness. Eventually he'd extracted everything that Sheldon knew about Sean's arrest.

"It is a ticklish problem, old top," said The Brain. "But you can rest assured that we will do our utmost to ensure Sean's freedom!"

He bent back over the leg.

"Observe the bite marks once more, Sheldon. Does anything strike you about them?"

Sheldon peered closely at Biff's leg.

"OK," he said. "I see the bite marks. Small bite marks. So what?"

The Brain gave him a cool look and sucked ruminatively on his unlit pipe.

"Is it not obvious to you, my dear Sheldon, that these bite marks couldn't possibly have been made by a crocodile?"

"Maybe some rats, or something like that, fancied a snack when the leg was in the river?"

"These small bites were not administered postmortem, Sheldon."

Sheldon looked at him blankly.

The Brain sighed.

"The small bites happened *before* the leg got in the river. *Before* Biff Manly was dead."

Sheldon goggled.

"That means that, that..."

The Brain nodded sagely and finished Sheldon's sentence.

"...that it wasn't the crocodile who was responsible for Manly's demise. Precisely, Sheldon."

"If it wasn't the croc that got Biff, what did?"

"That is the question, old top, that is the question. It's true that Mavis here certainly did contribute some damage to Mr. Manly's thigh bone. It takes a great deal of force to chop through a bone of that—I say, are you feeling all right, my good fellow?"

The Brain broke off from his cheery discussion of leg-chomping to watch Sheldon puke into the wastepaper bin. No sooner had Sheldon finished and lifted his head groggily from the bin, than The Brain began again.

"As I was saying, Mavis very likely did the bone damage, but I am as clear as I can be that she was most definitely not the cause of Mr. Manly's death. I am convinced, too, that your brother did not kill Biff Manly in a fight. The mere fact that he is relatively unscathed is evidence of that. No, I think that Mr. Manly was killed by some sort of gang."

"Gang?"

"The sheer number of bites, and the small size of those bites, means that whatever attacked Manly had to be small, perhaps the size of a small child or a person of limited height."

"Let me get this right," said Sheldon. "You're saying that Biff was knocked off by a gang of bloodthirsty toddlers? Or maybe a mob of murdering midgets? And not by the dirty great lump of meat-eating killer crocodile you found right next to the leg?"

The dirty great lump of meat-eating crocodile sat quietly on the floor playing with a rubber ball.

"I think the toddlers and the midgets are a little wide of the mark, Sheldon, but otherwise you have it correct. Manly *was* killed by a large number of small creatures. I've been out to the quarry for myself and there were a number of things I noticed that the police had missed. Manly was found face down in the creek that runs through and out of Henderson's Quarry. The police had examined everything around there very thoroughly, it's true; Snook isn't a complete imbecile. However, at the top of Henderson's Quarry I discovered a large number of small footprints which told an interesting story. An abandoned metal box gave me some more information. The water damage to Manly's leg told me something else. All of it contributed to one particular explanation *and one only*. But I'm confusing you. Perhaps it'd be better if I simply told you exactly what I now *think* happened out there..."

Chapter 11

*B*iff Manly grunted slightly as he hoisted the metal collection box out of his dusty Billabong bag and set it down in a small clearing in the trees above Henderson's Quarry. He looked around carefully. It was a hidden spot up here, the trees thick and tall, but you could never tell when one of those nosy park rangers would appear. Knowing his luck, it'd be just as he got this little beaut open.

"Farrago Bay Tsunami Fundraiser" read the label on the box. Biff had rocked up smooth as you like and boosted it right off the counter at The Pig in a Poke on the Creekside Beach boardwalk. He smirked as he recalled the tourists he'd seen stuffing the box with notes and coins in the past couple of weeks.

"Suckers," he smiled, and grabbed the crowbar from the bag at his feet. Biff put the edge of the bar into the ridge between the lip of the box and its lid, and pressed down. The crowbar slipped and tore a small gash in the fleshy part of Biff's hand where the thumb meets the palm. Fat drops of blood splashed onto the toes of his battered runners.

Biff swore loudly and jigged up and down. He waved his hand, sending blood drops splashing into the bushes. He kicked the side of the box and swore again as his big toe hit the metal.

This was going to take a little longer than expected.

Before Biff could take another try with the crowbar there was a small rustle from the trees about five meters away. Biff straightened up quickly and covered the box with his bag, his senses tingling, adrenaline surging through his nervous system. He held still a few moments, his head on one side. The sound had stopped. Biff shook his head, took up the crowbar again and bent to his task. This damn box was proving trickier to get open than he'd imagined.

Biff huffed and struggled with the crowbar.

"Bloody stupid bo—"

Biff broke off again and froze. There was more noise coming from the bush behind him and to his right, no mistake this time. Biff whirled around, convinced it was the police or the rangers or some other nosey parker come to muck things up for him. He tightened his grip on the crowbar.

A small koala stepped out of the greenery and sat down on the grass. It cocked its head, sniffed the air, and looked at Biff with button-black eyes, white teeth gleaming in the growing dusk. Biff blew out his breath, relieved.

"You put the willies up me good and proper, dude,"
he said. "Not right, sneakin' up on a bloke like that."

The koala looked at Biff and made a soft noise, half-snore, half-belch. Biff bent down, found a cricket-ball-

sized lump of rock and hurled it at the koala. To Biff's surprise the koala didn't dive back into the bushes. Instead it gave a low growl and moved closer. That was a bit...weird. Biff had never heard of a koala doing anything except eat, poo, and sleep. Come to think of it, he'd never seen a koala in the wild before, except on a school trip to Brisbane years ago.

"Now there's a thing," whispered Biff to himself.

He picked up another rock and this time took more care with his aim. He was going to crock the little fur ball a good one and no mistake, koala protection laws or not. Biff flexed his surfer muscles and threw the rock straight at the koala. He knew as soon as the rock left his hand that he'd nailed it. A perfect throw, straight and hard and fast. The rock flew toward the little animal like a bullet.

"Eat that, fur ball!" grunted Biff.

The koala caught the rock in its little black hands and lobbed it straight back at Biff as hard, or even harder than, Biff had thrown it. It hit Biff clean on the forehead and more of Biff's blood fell to the ground.

Biff reeled, flabbergasted. He propped himself up unsteadily on one hand, the other gingerly probing his head, which was flowing with blood.

"Jeez!" he gasped, hardly managing to understand what had just happened.

The koala reared up on its back legs and sniffed the air. Then, as the blood dripped from Biff's forehead, the koala dropped back on all fours and galloped toward him at a speed Biff wouldn't have believed possible if he hadn't seen it for himself. When the koala reached a spot just a couple of meters away, it sprang at Biff's throat, spitting and snarling. Gobs of drool hung in ribbons from its mouth. Biff caught a glimpse of a row of tiny square shining white teeth and wild black eyes ringed with red.

"What the—?"

Biff squealed in terror and batted blindly at the koala as it leaped toward him. He caught it a good one on the side of the head and the koala dropped to the ground, where it sat for a second before shaking its head and looking up at Biff, an expression of pure hatred on its face.

"Wait—," said Biff, but the koala bounced back up at him making a noise that made Biff's bowels turn to water. He turned and ran. It was obvious that the koala couldn't match him for speed.

Scared and angry, adrenaline throbbing into his overloaded nervous system, Biff shouted over his shoulder as he got a precious couple of yards between him and the koala. His breath came in great ragged waves of fear and he increased his speed across the clearing, his only thought to get away from the blood-crazed koala.

He had forgotten about the unopened charity box sitting in the center of the clearing.

Biff stumbled over it and hit the ground with a sickening crash.

In an instant the koala was on him. With an inhuman screech it sank its two front teeth into Biff's forearm. Biff howled.

"Flamin' Ada!" he screamed hysterically, scrambling back to his feet and waving the koala around in an attempt to shake it loose. It might as well have been grafted onto his arm for all the effect the shaking was having. The thing clung on, its teeth and claws digging trails of blood into Biff's forearm, its legs flying out behind it as Biff whirled and screamed. They spun in the middle of the forest clearing like an out-of-control merry-go-round.

Biff had never seen anything like it in his life. A killer koala!

Killer or not, thought Biff, his initial panic fading slightly, this koala was still punching well outside its weight. For god's sake, it was only a flaming koala! Then the thought that it might have rabies forced Biff into desperate action.

With an effort, Biff grabbed hold of the animal with his free hand. Ignoring the bites and scratches from the hissing ball of fury, he jerked it free and hurled it into the bushes. There was a satisfying crunch, followed by a silence, broken only by Biff's rasping breath.

"That'll teach ya to mess with—"

Biff stopped in midsentence as the bushes rustled.

Three koalas stepped out from the cover of the trees and into the clearing. One of them was clearly the one that had just had hold of Biff's arm. It was making noises to the other koalas and pointing at Biff. There were a series of dull thuds from behind Biff. He turned to see eight or nine koalas dropping from the trees, looking straight at him. Their teeth gleamed savagely in the darkening clearing, and Biff whimpered as they growled, drool dripping from their mouths.

Biff took a step to his right and the koalas matched

him. He took a step to the left and they fanned out in a circle around him. More koalas were arriving on the scene and they pressed slowly forward. There must have been thirty, forty, fifty of them. The growling grew into a rumble, louder and louder as they drew closer.

Biff sucked up whatever courage there was left in his massively depleted stock and made one big desperate effort to hurdle the first row of koalas.

He didn't make it, and with a howl of fury, the pack of killer koalas was on him. It was the last sound Biff would ever hear.

He didn't stand a chance.

Chapter 12

K iller koalas?"

The Brain nodded.

"That's your big theory? Biff was killed by a gang of koala bears on a bloodthirsty rampage?"

"Yet again," said The Brain, "you have summed up the situation with customary precision, my dear Sheldon. My latest theory is indeed that the unfortunate Mr. Manly was set upon by a pack of deranged koalas. Although I must correct your notion that koalas are bears. They belong to the marsupial family."

There was nothing really to be said, thought Sheldon. The Brain had plainly been working too hard lately or something, because this was just about the dumbest thing he'd ever heard.

"Koala bears—sorry, I mean koalas—just *don't* gang up on people, and they certainly don't rip surfers to shreds and dump their bodies in Henderson's Quarry!"

The Brain looked calm. He didn't appear to be worried by how stupid his theory sounded.

"You are quite correct, Sheldon, when you say that koalas do not, as a rule, launch fatal attacks on the general population. Neither do they normally work as an organized team of assassins. However, I am quite certain my theory is completely accurate."

He looked so smug, standing there waving his pipe around, that Sheldon felt he had to argue the point.

"C'mon, man!" he shouted. "This koala theory has to be just about as crazy as—"

The Brain looked meaningful at him. "As crazy as a saltwater crocodile thinking it's a dog?" he said.

Sheldon had to admit The Brain did have a point. "But how did you work out all that stuff about Manly?"

"Manly's movements are easily traced backwards from where he was found...*if* one knows what one is looking for. Snook and his men had, of course, examined the ground at the top of the cliff and noted the signs of a struggle. I believe that Manly fought with the koalas to the edge of the quarry cliff before falling, or possibly being thrown, to his death. No doubt the police came to a similar conclusion. The difference is that they only considered the possibility of a *human* struggle. They also did not fully trace Manly's movements back through the woods above the quarry, they did not find the collection box, and, crucially, they did not consider that his leg had been removed by a crocodile *after* he'd died. Mavis took Manly's leg and stored it in an underwater larder, as is the habit of crocodiles. That's why the leg had further evidence of water damage and why it was found further down the creek where the water is deeper. The leg must have bobbed up from Mavis's storage spot; perhaps it had been disturbed by some other aquatic creature. The point is that all of my conclusions follow Holmes's Law of Possibilities."

"Come again?" said Sheldon.

"Sherlock Holmes," said The Brain by way of explanation, pointing to the bookshelf. "When all other options have been excluded and only one conclusion is possible, then that explanation, no matter how unlikely, must be the truth. Simple logic."

"Still sounds weird," said Sheldon

"Let me show you something else," said The Brain. "Something that may convince you we are on the right track."

Twenty minutes later the two were a long way from The Brain's bedroom. They had slipped out across the flat garage roof and down a handily placed ladder.

"Couldn't we come back in daylight?" said Sheldon. "I'm freaked out enough with that koala story without wandering about out here at night."

"Please be patient, old top. There are very good reasons why we need darkness. Firstly, we have been able to shake off the person who has been following us—"

"What do you mean 'the person who has been following us?'" squeaked Sheldon. "Has someone been following us? Who?"

The Brain waved a hand airily.

"It is of no matter right now, dear boy. We have, I

am glad to say, already managed to shake him off. The darkness makes it difficult to follow someone successfully, you see? And, as I was saying before you interrupted, there is another reason why we are here at night: our friends don't do these activities in daylight."

"Who we meeting? Dracula?"

Sheldon wouldn't have put it past The Brain to be pals with The Forces of Darkness. Perhaps *that* was why he kept moving schools: he needed fresh supplies of blood. Maybe, thought Sheldon, his idea about human sacrifices wasn't so wide of the mark. Maybe *that* was why The Brain had hold of Biff's leg! Sheldon shivered, and not just because of the cool breeze. The Brain couldn't possibly be a blood-sucking creature of the night, could he? He *was* extremely pale, as if he spent his spare daylight hours inside a coffin, but Sheldon didn't feel he could come right out and ask him. If Sheldon couldn't work up the courage to ask The Brain about Mooloolaba, what chance did he have of getting The Brain to admit he was a vampire?

Sheldon shook his head. Dumb theory.

The Brain put his finger to his lips and frowned at Sheldon to be quiet, almost as if he had heard what was going on in Sheldon's head. Sheldon wondered if he'd spoken out loud. He was under severe mental pressure, after all, what with severed legs, killer koalas, canine crocs, and The Brain. Sheldon pulled himself together and took a look around.

It was late now, and the newest detectives in Farrago Bay were about a kilometer south down Creekside Beach Road. The Brain signaled to Sheldon and they dropped into the lane that ran behind a small row of shops facing the beach. It was almost pitch black there, and Sheldon had difficulty following The Brain as he ducked into the sports field at the back of the shops. The Brain grabbed hold of Sheldon and the two hunkered down behind a large tree.

"What are we doing here?" said Sheldon.

The Brain reached into his backpack and handed something to Sheldon.

"Here," The Brain said, "put these on. Night vision goggles."

Sheldon shrugged and slipped them on. He'd never worn night vision goggles before. There was a moment of absolute darkness and then Sheldon found the Farrago Bay night had turned an eerie milky green and white. Sheldon had seen enough news footage from war zones to know what night vision looked like, but it was different actually wearing the goggles. It took some getting used to and Sheldon could feel the beginnings of a headache.

The Brain, also wearing goggles, nudged him and pointed toward the back of the small supermarket.

"The supermarket?" said Sheldon. "What do we do now?"

The Brain put his finger to his thin lips.

"We wait."

Time passed slowly and Sheldon's headache got worse. He folded his arms and sat back against the trunk of the tree. He was cold. It was uncomfortable. A large pink rabbit dressed in scuba diving gear and carrying a rocket launcher passed by, and Sheldon realized he must have drifted off to sleep. He woke with a jerk to find The Brain gently shaking him.

"Sheldon," he whispered. "Sheldon! Wake up! They're here."

He pointed at the supermarket.

Sheldon adjusted his night vision goggles and looked. Behind one of the dumpsters several large figures were moving. Even with the goggles it was hard to pick them out as more than vague green blurs. Sheldon could hear muffled noises and clicks and an odd thumping sound. Then the frame of a window was pried open and a strangely shaped figure with elongated feet wiggled itself through the gap.

"Thieves!" gasped Sheldon.

Beside him The Brain nodded.

"Correct, dear boy," he said. "And pretty good ones too, by the look of it."

Sheldon looked again. Through the open window came box after box of goodies. A pair of thin arms held out each box before dropping it into the waiting arms of another thief below. Sheldon adjusted the focus on his goggles. There was something very odd about the thieves but, from where he was, Sheldon couldn't put his finger on exactly what.

"Shouldn't we get the police?" said Sheldon.

"Perhaps," said The Brain, "although I'm not sure Sergeant Snook would know how to deal with these *particular* criminals."

He pointed toward the dumpsters. The thieves, four of them Sheldon could now see, had finished their night's work. Laden down with armfuls of booty they bounced athletically out of the supermarket car park and across the sports field just thirty meters from Sheldon and The Brain.

"Kangaroos!" hissed Sheldon. "They're kangaroos!"

He was right. The thieves stood in the middle of the paddock, unaware that they were being watched, and ripped open the stolen boxes. They stuffed bags of crisps and boxes of doughnuts into their pouches before bounding into the woods and out of sight.

Sheldon turned to The Brain.

"OK, what was all that about? And how did you know they were going to be here? And what's all this got to do with Biff Manly? You don't think the kangaroos joined up with the koalas and killed him as well, do you? Sort of a cute animal gang thing?"

The Brain shook his head.

"No, not the kangaroos, although believe me that is a theory I considered. An attack by kangaroos, especially criminally minded kangaroos, could indeed have done for the unfortunate Mr. Manly. However, I think that, had kangaroos been involved there would have been more evidence of large scale bruising on Manly's leg. The feet, you see: kangaroos have extremely large feet. Besides, my observations indicate that the kangaroos are more interested in theft than violence. You may have heard of the burglary at the bakery last week. No? Thieves managed to scale a high security fence without the aid of a ladder. My deduction that kangaroos were involved was encouraged when I discovered droppings underneath the supermarket rear window. It was clear that something like this was in the air. As you have observed, my theory was correct."

He looked directly at Sheldon, the moonlight glancing off his goggles.

"And I am certain that the strange behavior of the kangaroos *is* linked to what happened with Mavis—"

"Who?" said Sheldon, confused for a moment. "Oh, the croc, yes."

"The crocodile, I was sure, would not be the only animal acting in a peculiar manner. And, since Mavis was in the same water as Mr. Manly's leg, I am convinced that there must be a link between the leg and the crocodile. Although not the one that Snook imagines."

Sheldon was about to say something when a flashing light lit up the night sky. He took off his night vision goggles and watched as a police car, its lights on but with the siren silent, accelerated along the coast road.

"Someone's in a hurry," said Sheldon. "Maybe it's the Chief of the Killer Koalas late for a meeting with the King Kangaroo."

"Most amusing, Sheldon. You must pass that one along to Sean the next time you visit him in jail. Now, if you don't have any further comedy routines, I suggest we investigate just where the police have turned their attention. Events are unfolding more rapidly than I imagined and time is of the essence! We haven't a moment to lose!"

He turned and began walking back in the direction of Sunshine Ridge. Sheldon sighed. This sidekick business was harder than it looked.

Chapter 13

A fat yellow moon lit up the road ahead of Sheldon and The Brain as they trudged toward the flashing blue lights, which could be glimpsed through the trees. The Brain had been silent on the walk back, and Sheldon hoped he wasn't still annoyed about that kangaroo joke. Maybe he was just thinking. He certainly did an awful lot of that. More than most people from Mooloolaba anyway, thought Sheldon. Although, to be fair, he hadn't met many Mooloolabians (could that really be what people from Mooloolaba were called?) and for all he knew the population of Mooloolaba was stuffed with Nobel Prize winners or rocket scientists or something equally brainy. One thing was for sure: Sheldon was beginning to doubt that that was where The Brain came from, school records or no school records.

The Brain's English accent seemed accurate, too, if old-fashioned. Not that Sheldon had had much experience with English people, but he did watch "The Bill" and "Inspector Morse" on TV from time to time, which was better than nothing, he supposed.

By the time they arrived at Sunshine Ridge it was almost midnight. As they reached the foot of Dibdob Lane, they stopped dead.

"Oh," said The Brain. "This is most unfortunate."

Three police cars and a bicycle were parked outside The Brain's house. This meant that the entire Farrago Bay police force was there. A large national park truck was there too, parked at an odd angle, its doors open as if the driver had not had time to close it before going inside. Radios crackled from the cars.

Every light in The Brain's house was on and the building throbbed with noise: shouting, banging, glass crashing. Despite the late hour, most of the neighborhood had come out to see what all the fuss was about and, Sheldon noted, pretty much everyone seemed to be having a whale of a time. He even spotted his mother sitting on a lawn chair sharing a mug of coffee with her gossip second-in-command, Mrs. Peckhammer. She must have been given the nod that there was top-class gawking to be had round at Dibdob Drive. Sheldon caught a small movement in the trees set back in one of the gardens. Peering more closely he saw a blond man sitting in the shadows on a deck reading a newspaper.

"What?" said The Brain, catching Sheldon's glance toward the shadows.

"Nothing," said Sheldon. "Just a bloke reading the newspaper."

"Interesting," said The Brain. "Reading a newspaper in the dark is an uncommon skill, don't you think, Sheldon?"

Sheldon gasped. "You mean that's the guy who's been following us?"

Before The Brain could reply, a piercing scream cut through the night air and the front door of The Brain's house flew open. Three things then happened in quick succession.

A screaming woman who Sheldon recognized as The Brain's mother (or at least as the silent woman he'd seen in The Brain's house) burst from the house and sped off down Dibdob Drive.

Next, four more figures popped out of the house like corks from a bottle and scrambled for footholds on the damp grass. The first was a man who looked like he worked for the National Park Ranger Service. He had a beard and wore lots of green, so Sheldon thought he was on fairly safe ground with that assumption. He also carried a large tranquilizer rifle. The park ranger sprinted from the doorway dragging a broken net behind him and wailing like a baby. He ran off and disappeared into the inky blackness. Next came the other three members of the Farrago Bay police force all (in Sheldon's opinion) yodeling like complete nellies. Sheldon was pretty sure the last one was asking for his mummy as he ran past.

Finally, through the door came a dark familiar shape wagging a heavy tail from side to side.

"Mavis," murmured Sheldon.

"I say, old top," said The Brain, squinting through his spectacles and nudging Sheldon with a sharp elbow. "It looks to me like she's got something in her mouth."

Sheldon peered toward where Mavis stood on the lawn.

"Yes, you're right. It looks like she's carrying something."

As they watched, Mavis stepped forward and came into range of Mr. Livercock's security light, which snapped on in a blaze, lighting her up like an actress on stage. There was a moment of stunned disbelief before the inhabitants of Dibdob Drive realized there was a large crocodile on the loose and immediately went completely bananas.

Mrs. Peckhammer became entangled in her lawn chair and fell to the ground yelling for help. Sheldon's mother accidentally trod on Mrs. Peckhammer's head as she launched herself, with impressive agility, up the nearest tree like an orangutan with its rear end on fire. Babbling hysterically, Mrs. Peckhammer tried to dig her way under her own lawn using her teeth. Everywhere Sheldon looked people were diving through hedges, jumping back into their houses, locking doors, climbing onto porches. Sheldon saw one man dive into his pool before realizing that probably wasn't a good place to escape from a crocodile. He jumped out again and ran straight into the wooden pole of a poolside tiki hut, knocking himself out cold.

In the chaos, Sheldon and The Brain were the only people moving toward the crocodile.

"Um, do you think we should be heading the other way, Brain?" Sheldon asked, only to find that The Brain wasn't listening. Sheldon was more than a little worried that Mavis might have decided that being a dog was a little *tame* and had taken up full-time crocodiling again. The Brain obviously didn't share his opinion.

"Mavis!" he shouted and waved at the crocodile. She turned toward his voice and for the first time they got a clear view of what she was carrying.

It was Sergeant Snook.

Mavis held him gently, but firmly, around the middle, his hands trapped by his sides. He seemed to be in one piece as far as they could tell. His legs waved pathetically around, one shoe hanging off. His eyes bulged. Well, Sheldon figured, they would, wouldn't they?

"You!" he said, catching sight of The Brain.

"Ah," said The Brain. "Sergeant Snook."

"Is that the best you can do?" yelled Snook. "Ooh! You are in *so* much trouble, young feller-*erk*!"

Snook "erked" because Mavis, seeing The Brain, gave a muffled bark and ran straight up the street toward him. Sheldon bravely stood right behind The Brain, ready to throw him to Mavis if she turned out to have gone nuts after all. Then a sudden thought struck him like a cold bucket of water. What was he talking about "if" she was nuts? The croc thought she was a dog, for crying out loud! She'd already *gone* nuts.

Crazy or not, Sheldon made sure he was still safely behind The Brain when Mavis lumbered up and stopped in front of him.

She opened her jaws and dropped Snook on the road. He bounced a little on the tarmac and lay there snorting heavily. Sheldon could see Snook really wanted to lay into The Brain, but the fact that he was in the company of a nine-hundred-kilo killing machine cooled him on this idea for the time being. However, Sheldon could tell from the way Snook's face was turning red that he was storing up some serious revenge against The Brain.

If he survived. And at the moment that didn't seem very likely.

Mavis wagged her big tail awkwardly (her tail wasn't designed for wagging but she was giving it her best shot) and knocked over a couple of garbage bins sitting outside number seventy-six. She barked and a few of the more nervous types left in Dibdob Drive squealed. Sheldon was one of them.

"Sorry," he said. "I'd forgotten she did that."

"Get me out of here!" yelled Snook, his face turning an even less flattering shade of red.

The Brain looked thoughtful, considering the situation. Then—Sheldon could almost hear the connections being made inside his head—he brightened and lifted a finger in triumph.

He looked down at Snook like someone who'd discovered the secret of the universe.

"She thinks you're a stick," said The Brain.

"*What*? You *what*? A *what*? She thinks I'm a *what*?" said Snook, clearly not believing his ears.

"A *stick*, my good fellow," said The Brain, pronouncing every letter crisply. "Mavis thinks you're a stick."

Snook's eyeballs, already bulging like squeezed balloons, managed to bulge just a little more.

"Who's *Mavis*, fer cryin' out loud?" he squeaked. "And why does she think I'm a *stick*? I don't even *look* like a stick!"

"Well, actually…" Sheldon started to say, but Snook cut him off with a glare.

The Brain pointed at the crocodile.

"My apologies, Sergeant Snook, where are my manners? This is Mavis, Sergeant. Mavis, this is Sergeant Snook."

"Pleased to meet y—" said Snook, starting to hold out a hand toward Mavis before remembering she was a crocodile. "Now wait a minute, young feller, never mind all that rubbish! What do you mean 'this is Mavis?' And what's all that 'stick' nonsense?"

The Brain sighed. Policemen.

"It is perfectly simple, Sergeant," he said in a voice you might use to explain the workings of a toilet to a three-year-old. "Mavis is the crocodile in front of you. Mavis thinks she's a dog. Dogs chase sticks. Mavis thinks you are a stick, or at least will do until a real stick turns up. *Ergo,* my firm advice would be to pretend to *be* a stick until we can find a way to distract her."

"I'm *not* a stick!" shouted Snook indignantly. "And I wouldn't know how to pretend to be a stick! What's more, I absolutely, point-blank refuse to pretend to be a st—"

It's amazing the effect that a bite, even a small one, from a fully grown crocodile will have on stubborn policemen. Just one tiny nip on Snook's bony rear end and he was impersonating sticks like his life depended upon it. Which it might have. Who could predict what a crocodile-dog with an identity crisis would do next?

If Sheldon lived to be a million years old he was sure he would never witness anything as downright hilarious as the next few minutes of Snook pretending to be a stick.

Have you ever tried to be a stick? Neither has anyone else in the history of the world. It's not something that comes naturally, except maybe to certain old ladies, and you couldn't say they were actually *trying* to be sticks. Even a very good mime would be hard pushed to come up with a convincing impersonation of a length of wood. But with Mavis's encouragement, Snook really put his heart and soul into it. First he went stiff and started saying (through gritted teeth) "I'm a stick! I'm a stick!" Sheldon nearly cried with laughter. He wished he'd had a camera.

"C'mon then, you big lump!" snarled Snook at Mavis. "Can't you see I'm a bloody stick?"

Mavis didn't understand what was going on at first and, for a hairy moment, it looked to Sheldon that she may have decided to cut her losses and eat the stringy policeman lying on the road. The Brain stepped in and pretended to throw Snook. He made a throwing motion; Snook rolled away from him, looking as stick-like as humanly possible (which, Sheldon had to admit, wasn't really much). Still, it seemed enough to convince Mavis and that was, after all, the point of the exercise.

From that point on it was plain sailing. Unless you were Snook, of course, because, even with Mavis trying to be gentle, there was inevitably a certain amount of wear and tear on Snook's person. The odd ripped sweater here, a grazed elbow there. But, as Sheldon watched, he knew it was the sheer humiliation of pretending to be a stick that was the most painful thing of all for Snook.

Sheldon loved every minute of it.

But, like all good things, it eventually came to an end. For Mavis the end took the shape of the reappearance of the bearded park ranger. He had recovered his nerve enough to come back with his tranquilizer rifle.

"You took your ruddy time, Don!" said Snook savagely from where he lay firmly wedged between Mavis's jaws. She dropped him at The Brain's feet and he "threw" Snook one more time. Snook clamped his hands to his sides once more and, keeping his legs as close together as possible, rolled his way across the street. Sheldon had to admit, he was now doing an excellent job of impersonating a stick.

"Fetch!" yelled The Brain. Mavis gave a gleeful bark and lolloped after Snook.

"What's the idea, Bill?" said the ranger, clearly astonished at the sight of Snook rolling across the road.

"He's pretending to be a stick," Sheldon said helpfully.

"A *stick*?" said Don, his eyebrows disappearing into his park ranger hat. "What's he pretending to be a stick for? Doesn't he know we're trying to deal with a dangerous animal? What a waste of time."

"Never mind all that, you flaming great bearded idiot!" howled Snook. "Shoot the bloody thing!"

The ranger grumbled something about it not being right for certain blokes to be disrespectful about other blokes' flaming beards especially when they could remember a time not so long ago when certain blokes had flaming great nelly mustaches drooping halfway down past their flaming chins, before lifting the rifle to his shoulder and shooting a dart into Mavis's side.

Mavis paused, Snook wedged in her mouth, and staggered a little. She gave an almighty grunt and then, before anyone could react, raced off into the dark bush at about a hundred kilometers an hour.

"*Hel-l-l-l-p!*" wailed Snook as the two disappeared from view.

"Crikey!" said the bearded ranger, clearly not expecting Mavis to be able to run after being hit by a tranquilizer dart. "That's not good."

There was more distant screaming from Snook and then a muffled splash as though a crocodile-dog-police-man-stick combination had jumped into Coldcut Creek and swum off. Which, curiously enough, was exactly what had happened.

"Hmm," said The Brain, replacing his pipe between his teeth. "Most singular."

Sheldon looked at him. "Singular" didn't come close. There was going to be hell to pay for this one.

Chapter 14

The morning after the night before. It had been a strange night, thought Sheldon, especially by the standards of Farrago Bay. It had been a pretty eventful night by the standards of *anywhere*, with the possible exception of certain districts of Los Angeles, Mexico City, or Kowloon on a particularly heavy Saturday night. Sheldon sat up in bed and tried to collect his thoughts.

To briefly recap, what had happened so far was:

The murder, or manslaughter (of Biff) by person or persons unknown.

The arrest of Sean for murder.

The discovery of the missing leg.

The theory of the killer koalas.

The thieving kangaroos.

Last, but by no means least, there was the Mavis Snook-chewing incident.

"If I've missed anything out—and I'm sure I have—," Sheldon sighed to himself.

He sank back into the pillows and groaned. His head was whirling with questions.

What happened to Snook? Did Mavis eat him? What was going to happen next?

He didn't have long to wait. The doorbell rang, and shortly afterwards, Sheldon was taken down to the station by PC Higgins for a spot of questioning.

They made him wait in a cell next door to Sean, which cheered Sean up considerably.

"Haw haw!" he laughed through the bars. "Bagged another McGlone, eh? Haw haw haw!"

Sheldon noticed there was only one empty cell left. If, for example, his mother didn't get any cigarettes that day, Snook would end up with the jail stuffed to the limit with the entire McGlone family, because she would surely kill him.

On the whole, Sheldon hoped Snook hadn't been eaten. Much as he disliked him, Sheldon didn't think Snook deserved to be eaten alive. Apart from anything else, it would mean more problems for the McGlones.

The door to the cell swung open.

It was Snook.

Last seen proceeding in a northerly direction toward Coldcut Creek, clamped firmly in Mavis's jaws, Snook had not, as most people had naturally assumed, perished. Instead, completely intact (or at least with both his arms and legs still attached), here he was, standing in front of Sheldon with the look of A Man with a Grudge.

Snook, Sheldon discovered later, had turned up wet,

dirty, bruised, and very, very cross indeed after spending a long half hour as Mavis's chew toy before the tranquilizer dart eventually managed to put Mavis to sleep. Unfortunately for Snook, she had gone to sleep with him still in her mouth. It had taken him almost four hours to struggle out from between her sharp white teeth and make his way back through mosquito-infested swamp to Farrago Bay. Sheldon had to admit the experience had left its mark on Snook. He looked terrible.

Through a pair of mosquito-stung, red-rimmed eyes, Snook fixed Sheldon with a cold glare of concentrated hatred. His need to fix the blame on someone for his terrible night was powerful, and Sheldon had an idea that that blame might be heading his way. The slightly baffled, dumb-ish, faint-whiff-of-cabbage-about-him Snook had been replaced overnight by an evil, vindictive, croc-chewed Snook from whom all trace of humanity had been snuffed.

It didn't matter to this new Snook that Sheldon was the youngest offspring of the love of his life, nor that Sheldon had not actually had anything to do with Mavis, or the leg (officially at any rate). No, it was enough that Sheldon was, as Snook put it, a known associate of one Theophilus Brain of 54 Dibdob Drive, in whose bedroom both Mavis and the leg had been hidden.

Snook's first choice for a proper going-over had been The Brain, of course, but The Brain was nowhere to be found. The last time Sheldon had seen him was the previous night.

"Looks like a spot of lying-low may be called for, old top." he said. "I'm relying on you to stand firm, keep your chin up, and play with a straight bat. I'm going undercover. Pip, pip."

And with that he had slipped off into the darkness, leaving Sheldon to face the music.

"You and that egghead mate of yours have got some explaining to do, sonny," snarled Snook in a low rumble. "I want answers."

Snook leaned forward until his purple-bruised lip was millimeters from Sheldon.

"And I want them now. Got it?"

Sheldon nodded, his upper lip curling in a sneer. This copper could ask all he liked; Sheldon was going to make like a clam, say nothing, button it, keep it zipped.

Two minutes later Sheldon was quite surprised to find he had confessed all about Biff's leg being in The Brain's bedroom. Sheldon didn't know how Snook got it out of him: One minute he was sitting there saying nothing—*nada, absolutamundo rien,* you'll never get it outta me, copper, his mouth zipped as tight as a corked bottle—the next minute he'd blurted out everything. Proper policemen, as Sheldon found, even doughnut munchers like Snook, could look at you in a way that makes you think you *must* have done something terrible, and made you start to think it'd be a good idea to tell them something, *anything,* to keep them happy. You *wanted* to keep them happy, if only to stop them looking at you like that.

"Let me get this completely straight, Sheldon," said

Snook, perching one skinny hip on the corner of the desk, "you and Brain had Manly's leg up in his room all this time? What, did you forget about it? Easily done, I know, forgetting about body parts of murdered surfers and leaving them lying around. Could happen to anyone."

At that point there was a commotion in the corridor, followed by Sheldon's mother storming into the cell, Sean's lawyer Perelman close behind.

"*Hnmh flmmmb shh ambff,*" said Perelman looking up through a face-full of half-eaten muffin. He waved his hand while he cleared his mouth of muffin.

"My client doesn't have to answer that, Officer Snook," he said through a crumb-lined mouth, before spoiling the effect a little by adding, "I think."

"Oh, do shut up, Perce," said Snook.

"Um, OK," said Perelman. "Just thought I'd mention it."

He put his head down and crammed another chunk of muffin into his mouth.

"Perce?" said Sheldon's mother.

"Um, yup?" said Perelman.

"You're an idiot," she snapped and stubbed her cigarette out savagely on Snook's interview table. "You don't have to say a thing, Sheldon. Not without me and—God help us"—she looked sideways at Perelman—"your lawyer."

"That's all right, Mum. I want to put things straight. The Brain just wanted to help!" said Sheldon turning toward Snook, an imploring expression on his face. "He's absolutely brilliant at finding things out! He's got

117

one of the best detecting brains in the whole world, all because he...um...fell into the...er...Genius Machine thingamajig at the Institute in Zurich along with all those books and, um..."

Sheldon trailed off into silence. In the cold light of Farrago Bay police station it didn't sound too convincing, even to himself.

"Hold on," said Snook, a look on his face of a man who's just thought of something.

"There *was* no leg in that bedroom! All we found was that bloody croco—"

He stopped and everyone realized what must have happened at the same time. Snook turned purple.

"And you say this friend of yours is *clever,* eh? Not so ruddy clever that he didn't know what would happen if he left a leg in a small room with a large hungry croc, eh, hmm? What are we going to do now about that leg? It was an important piece of evidence, was that leg. Very, very important!"

It was also an important bit of Biff Manly, too, thought Sheldon, but he kept quiet while Snook huffed and puffed around the cell making little grunts of frustration. He'd have pulled his hair out if he'd had enough left.

"You pair of interfering little busybodies! You could have destroyed some important evidence by letting that croc—"

"Mavis," Sheldon said helpfully. "We call her Mavis."

"I don't care what her blasted name is! That ruddy croc ate Manly's ruddy leg!"

Snook paused, breathing heavily, his nostril hair bristling unattractively. He looked from Sheldon to his mother and then over to where Sean sat on a wooden bench watching wrestling on a small TV with wire over the screen.

Sheldon could see that Snook had thought of something. It was as if he could actually trace the thought process traveling (slowly, slowly) through Snook's brain and then emerging on his face in an expression of manic triumph that lit him up like a pinball machine.

"Wait just a minute, though!" said Snook. "Wait just a flea-bitten minute! I can see it all now, oh-ho, can I ever see it all now! You fellers were making sure that no one found out anything about that leg so that that no-good brother of yours would get off with cold-blooded murder!"

"Hoy!" said Mrs. McGlone. "That's my boy you're talking about, Bill!"

"I've told you before, Mary, it's 'Sergeant Snook' down at the station."

"Sergeant, Bill, Captain Flamin' Y-fronts, whatever it is you want to be called, that's still my boy you're calling a killer!"

"But—"

"No 'but' about it, *Bill,* that boy's no murderer and you know it! And if you can't see it, then you're dumber than I always thought you were—which is about as dumb as you can get without needing to be fed with a spoon, I can tell you!"

There was a moment's silence while Mrs. McGlone glared furiously at Snook and Snook changed color from red to white and then back to red again. He looked like a barber's pole. Sheldon wondered whether there was any chameleon DNA in Snook's family. Perce Perelman gawked and shuffled some papers in a pointless sort of way and nibbled on the remains of his muffin.

"Come on," said Mrs. McGlone, dragging Sheldon to his feet. "I'm taking you home. I've had about as much of this carry-on as I can take."

Snook still had plenty of questions, but there was something in Mary McGlone's expression that would have had better men than him thinking twice before piping up. Sheldon thought that even a full-grown grizzly bear might have hesitated.

Sensibly, Snook decided to quit while he still had one McGlone behind bars. Judging by the mood his mother was in, Sheldon wouldn't have put it past her to rip open the steel door with her teeth to get Sean and drag him home too. Instead, she barged past Snook with one final volcanic glare and led Sheldon out into the Farrago sun, pausing only to shout over her shoulder at Snook not to bother slinking round for a bite to eat that evening or any other evening, for that matter.

"We're gonna announce the arrest tomorrow, Mary! There's nothing you can do about that!" shouted Snook as the door closed behind the McGlones.

"Ah, blow it out yer ear, ya big galoot!" yelled Sheldon's mother over her shoulder.

"There's something else, Mary," shouted Snook. "We found some DNA evidence! Sean's hair was underneath Biff's fingernails! We got him and there's no wriggling out of it!"

"Hair?" said Mrs. McGlone, stopping in her tracks and turning to face him. "No one mentioned anything about hair before! That Annie Madison you had looking at Biff didn't find any hairs, or at least that's what you told me!"

"Not at first, she didn't, no," said Snook. "But after a second autopsy, kindly paid for by Mr. Horrocks, Sean's hairs were found. We had them tested and the tests say they're Sean's. It's a clear-cut case, Mary, clear-cut."

To Sheldon it smelt fishier than the hold of a deep-sea trawler, but it seemed good enough for Snook and the rest of the flatfoots.

Things were not looking good. For Sean, that was.

Where was The Brain when they needed him?

Chapter 15

The next morning The Pig in a Poke was packed with people from the press. Snook had called a media conference to announce the sensational solving of The Biff Manly Murder Mystery by himself and his crack squad of detectives. The station had been too small to squeeze in all the TV and press people, so The Pig in a Poke it was.

Snook stood on one of the small boxes that served as a temporary stage and looked out self-importantly at the crowd. Sitting behind a table on the stage with Snook were Mayor Badseed and Howard Horrocks, the Dent-O man. Sheldon wondered what *he* was doing there, apart from sticking his nasty interfering nose into other people's business.

As it was a Saturday, everyone who could manage to cram into The Pig was there. Sheldon even saw a rather tired-looking Miss Fleming scowling near the cash register. She caught Sheldon's eye and looked at him blankly. Strange, he thought, normally she'd cremate me from across the room with a single blast from her death-ray stare. Now she looked as though it would all be too much effort.

"Must have been up eating humans all night," Sheldon muttered to himself.

He looked out the window. Across the street two large fig trees shaded Farrago Bay's central street. A large number of black shapes wheeled erratically in the air above them. Sheldon looked closer. Bats. The fig trees were home to hundreds of fruit bats and they were a common sight around Farrago Bay.

Except they only fly at night, thought Sheldon. Don't they?

He wondered if The Brain had noticed the bats. If he was still around, that is. There was no doubt that he was onto something with his animal theories. Sheldon wondered what it was all about: Mavis, the kangaroos, The Brain's weird theory about the koalas...

Sheldon turned back to the room as Snook tapped the microphone. A gradual reduction of noise levels in the room signaled the start of the conference.

"Ladies and gentlemen, members of the press, thank you for coming," said Snook, beaming proudly.

"Buffoon," said a familiar voice close by Sheldon's ear. Sheldon jerked and looked around. A large dark-skinned man dressed in a sharp blue suit and wraparound black sunglasses was the only person close enough to have spoken. Sheldon looked closer, puzzled.

"Don't react, Sheldon old thing. It's *me!*" said The Brain's voice from behind a full beard. A porkpie hat was pulled down low over his eyes.

"I thought it was wise to conceal my identity. What do you think? Will it pass muster?"

Sheldon considered The Brain for a moment.

"You look...*different.*"

This was something of an understatement.

Somehow (and Sheldon was at a loss as to how exactly he had achieved it), The Brain had managed to add about two feet to his height and forty kilos to his weight. Even his head seemed smaller, more normal, wedged under the hat.

"I'm a reporter for Channel Z news," he said. "At least that's what I'm telling anyone who asks."

"Is there a Channel Z?" asked Sheldon.

"Of course not. But these days who would know? Even MTV has a news team."

Now that Sheldon knew it was The Brain it seemed impossible that no one else would notice his disguise, but it did seem to be working. True, there were a few whispered nudges toward the sharp-dressed reporter, but no one seemed to think it was The Brain in disguise. Least of all Snook, or any of the rest of Farrago Bay's finest, who were all busy preening themselves under the warm glow of publicity.

"I think you'll be OK," whispered Sheldon as Snook started speaking.

"I am delighted," said Snook, "to be able to announce the successful conclusion of our exhaustive investigation into the tragic murder of one of Farrago Bay's best-loved residents, Nigel 'Biff' Manly. Mr. Manly, as most of you will already have heard, was found in Henderson's Quarry. He had been pushed or thrown from the cliffs above the quarry after a violent fight. His leg had been removed after his death, possibly for some as-yet-undiscovered voodoo ritual. Following statements from witnesses, DNA evidence, and our own professional observations at the crime scene, yesterday we arrested a local youth, well-known to police, one Sean Aloysius McGlone, a roofer's mate aged seventeen years and nine months, on a charge of murder. McGlone was known to have argued violently with the deceased in the weeks leading up to his death. During a second postmortem examination, kindly paid for by Dent-O, we found DNA evidence linking McGlone to the deceased."

Sergeant Snook paused dramatically and took a sip of lemonade. He looked around the room to find the camera of the local TV station and stared right into the lens. He continued speaking in a deeply serious and sincere voice.

"The force used by McGlone in Mr. Manly's death was sickening, even to a hardened professional policeman like myself."

Snook sounded as though he'd spent the past twenty years patrolling the scarier parts of the Bronx rather than snoozing in his cruiser at the back of the Big W. Sheldon snorted loudly—he'd have harrumphed if he'd known how—and a few of the cleverer scribblers and snappers who knew Sheldon was related to the alleged murderer, turned and clicked cameras at him.

Snook continued.

"This crime was horrifying. The person responsible went absolutely berserk. Ab-so-lute-ly berko."

He stopped, pointed his finger out at the audience, and raised his voice dramatically. For a crazy moment

Sheldon thought he was about to burst into song.

"Which is why I pledge that the entire power of the Farrago Bay police department will be brought to bear to get the death penalty for Sean McGlone!" He nodded at the rest of the department—PCs Gary, Phil, and Ken— who were sitting around a small table off to one side. They all smiled appreciatively at Snook. Gary and Phil gave him the thumbs up. Ken looked a bit worried. He moved over and whispered something in Snook's ear.

Snook coughed.

"Um—thanks Ken," he said. "My colleague has just pointed out that we don't actually have the death penalty anymore in this state so, er, we'll have to see what we can do."

There was a brief pause before Snook recovered his poise and started speaking again.

"Biff's young life was snuffed out, right in his prime. We believe we have the evidence to gain a conviction. We have a motive: jealousy. We have forensic evidence: a DNA match for hairs found under the victim's finger-nails. We have a witness: the honorable Mr. Horrocks. In short, we have our man. That's about all we have for you today, folks. There will be a memorial board-off down at Creekside Beach in honor of Biff tomorrow, starting at three. The event has been kindly sponsored by Dent-O Toothpaste…"

"Now there's a surprise," said Sheldon, loudly enough for Snook to hear.

"Anyway," said Snook, after a nasty glance aimed in Sheldon's direction, "I'd like to say a big thanks to Mr. Horrocks of Dent-O, who'd like to add a few words."

Snook gave an oily smile and pointed to the microphone in case Horrocks had never seen one before. While Horrocks prattled away about Biff as if he'd been some kind of surfing Mother Teresa, The Brain held up a small mobile phone with a built-in camera and snapped a photo of him. With economical movements he plugged the phone into what looked like an old cornflake box (the mini kind that you get in those variety packs) with a keyboard attached, and began tapping away as Horrocks spoke. Sheldon looked over his shoulder and saw him type something in a search window. The cornflake box must have been satellite linked to the internet or something, because a whole bunch of information came up onscreen.

"Face Match," said The Brain quietly, his fingers flying across the keys.

"Face Match?"

"A bit of a kit I knocked together from this and that, my good fellow," said The Brain tapping the cornflake box affectionately. "This little fellow draws visual information from all known police computers and attempts to Face Match it with all known criminals on the planet. Very hit and miss, I admit, but sometimes one has a stroke of fortune."

The Brain tapped away. In the background Horrocks seemed to be coming to the end of his tribute to Biff. The Brain tapped Sheldon on the arm and pointed at the screen.

"Observe, my good fellow."

Onscreen a photo of Howard Horrocks blinked up. "Len 'Easy' Wimslow," read the caption. "Age forty-four, also known as 'Chemical' Wimslow or 'Lenny the Penny' Wimslow. Previous convictions: fraud, theft, food hygiene violations, impersonating a police officer, operating a business without a license…"

The list ran on and on.

"The guy's a crook! I knew it!" Sheldon hissed, loud enough for Horrocks to turn toward him.

"Well spotted, Sheldon old top," whispered The Brain. "But I would suggest you lower your decibel level. You may be alerting our foes."

"So what? Let's tell Snook now!" said Sheldon. "This Horrocks feller might…"

The Brain held up his hand.

"Not so fast, dear boy. Horrocks served time in jail for his crimes. He has paid his debt to society and cannot be touched."

Sheldon scratched his head.

"However," continued The Brain, "Mr. Horrocks *is* someone who we could do with looking at more closely. I feel a visit to Dent-O might be in order."

"You gonna order somethin' or wha'?"

They looked up to see Iggy, quite possibly the filthiest cook between Farrago Bay and Bilbao, and owner of The Pig in a Poke, scratching one of his chins. Sheldon asked for a Coke.

"How 'bout chew, big feller?" said Iggy, looking at The Brain.

The Brain shook his head "no" to the food and ordered a cup of tea. Iggy turned to annoy some reporters from the *Farrago Bay Bugle*. There was a Mrs. Iggy somewhere, Sheldon knew; he'd heard her shuffling around in the kitchen at The Pig, and sometimes caught a glimpse of a meaty hand sliding food through the hatch, but he'd never actually seen her. Sheldon looked at Iggy and thought perhaps it was just as well, all things considered.

Up on stage Snook was wrapping things up.

"...and in conclusion there will be a progress report as soon as my department has made some, um, progress. In the meantime, I think that all of our thoughts should be with poor Biff's family in this, their sad, sad time."

Snook looked to his left at Biff's dad, Ray.

"Our thoughts are with you, mate."

Ray Manly looked a bit nervous about being the center of attention and nodded.

"Now," said Snook. "Are there any questions?"

The reporters all started speaking at once.

"Is there a rogue crocodile on the loose?"

"What is the Farrago Bay police department doing to ensure public safety?"

"Is there any truth to the rumor that you intend to bring in marksmen to shoot the crocodile?"

"What can you tell us about reports that Mr. Manly's left leg is still missing?"

After Snook had finished waffling the answers, The Brain stood and raised his notebook. Snook nodded in his direction.

"Bertie Brickblock, Channel Z Special Crime Unit," said The Brain. "Sergeant Snook, is there any truth in the story that Dent-O has made a generous donation to the Farrago Bay Police Retirement Fund, on condition that there's a speedy wrap-up of the Biff Manly case?"

To Sheldon, The Brain sounded as much like a TV news reporter as a kookaburra sounds like the Queen of England, but Snook didn't seem to have noticed.

"Perhaps I could answer that last question," said Horrocks smoothly, his gleaming teeth moving toward the microphone like a shark toward a surfer. "While it is true that Dent-O are proud supporters of the magnificent job the Farrago Bay police men and women do on behalf of this community, there is absolutely no link between that support and this investigation. Dent-O has a proud record of serving the community wherever it is based, and Farrago Bay is no exception. Dent-O has been here for over two years now. We'd like to think that bringing more than two hundred and eighty jobs to this town shows exactly where Dent-O's heart lies!"

There was a round of applause from the audience. Sheldon noticed quite a few locals giving "Bertie Brickblock" the evil eye. Jobs were hard to come by in Farrago and there was no doubt that plenty of people had been glad of the work. Even his dad had been thinking of getting a job there, Sheldon remembered.

Sheldon noticed Fleming slip out the door.

"Come, Sheldon," said The Brain hurriedly, getting up from the booth and closing the lid on his cornflake-box-transmitter gadget. "Our work here is done."

Neither of them noticed Horrocks nod to a blond man standing at the back of The Pig. He slipped smoothly out behind Sheldon and The Brain.

They were being followed.

Chapter 16

At the same moment that Sheldon and The Brain were leaving The Pig, on the other side of town, two fishermen were looking forward to an afternoon on the water.

Bren, seated in the passenger seat of Bret's new Land Cruiser, rummaged around inside the tackle box on his lap and held up two brightly painted fishing lures.

"What do you reckon, mate?"

"I reckon it looks like too much hard work, mate," said Bret, glancing over the top of his milkshake. "All that casting out and winding back in. Nah, what I reckon is we stick a slice of mullet on the hooks, drop 'em over the side, suck down a couple of cold ones, and wait for the fish to come to us."

Bren put the lures back in the box and smiled.

"Sounds like a plan, mate," said Bret. "We don't want to wear ourselves out or nothing."

A mosquito landed on Bret's forearm and plunged its proboscis into his lobster-red skin. He slapped it awkwardly into a bloody smear, spilling a little of his shake on the buttery-soft leather of the brand new car. Cursing, Bret turned the Land Cruiser into the parking lot for the boat-ramp access and crunched to a halt a few centimeters from the water's edge, the snout of the car pointing out at the river.

"Flaming mosquitoes, mate! Don't know why we don't just nuke 'em like the Yanks do."

"The greenies don't like it, mate," said Bren, chuckling. "Now stop whinging and let's go fishing!"

Bret eased his considerable bulk out of the car, slurped down the last of his strawberry shake, and threw the empty cup into a nearby bush. He belched loudly and vigorously scratched under his arm. On the other side, Bren stepped out, farted, and stretched his arms out wide.

"Good day for it, mate."

"You said it, mate."

As they moved to unhook the trailer holding the boat, Bret appreciatively patted the polished metal roof of the new car.

"Nice motor you've got there, mate," said Bren. "You wanna look after it. Stop chucking milkshakes all over it."

"Thanks for the advice, mate, I will."

The fully loaded, top-of-the-range Land Cruiser was Bret's little reward to himself. Sort of a pat on the back after using cheap-rate concrete to finish the last of those miserable little units out on the spit of land by Burgess Beach.

Bren got the boat into the water and left the trailer

at the side of the ramp. Bret stepped aboard, the boat rocking wildly as he settled into place.

"You finished playing silly buggers, mate, or can we go fishing?" said Bren smiling toothlessly.

"Get in, you plank."

Bren jumped aboard and Bret puttered out into the river. He was about to gun the engine when a movement from the car caught his eye.

"What is it, mate?" said Bren. "Forget your beer?"

Bret pointed at the Land Cruiser. Someone was inside.

"There's some mongrel in me car, mate! Look!" Bret pointed toward his new car, outrage written all over his face. "I'll kill 'em!"

"You must have left the keys in, you muppet!" said Bren.

Bret turned the boat around quickly and pushed the throttle wide open, desperate to get back to his car. The boat immediately lifted its prow out of the water and capsized. The two men spluttered to the surface just as the Land Cruiser's engine roared into life.

"Oh, genius move, mate!" said Bren, pulling weeds from his mouth. "That'll really fool them!"

"Quick!" yelped Bret. "They're stealing the flaming thing!"

Bren stood chest deep in the river, motionlessly peering at the car.

"What are you standing here for?" panted Bret. "Come on!"

Bren put his finger to his lips and jerked a thumb toward the car.

"There's loads of them, mate!" he hissed. "Might be more than we can handle."

Bret looked. Bren was right. Six or seven small heads were bobbing about inside the cab. It looked like a gang.

"Bloody kids, mate!" he snapped. "We can handle them! Let's go!"

He waved a fist at the car. "Oi!" he shouted.

Bren clamped a hand over Bret's mouth. "Wait, mate!" he whispered. "There's something not right about this. Take a closer look."

Bret waddled to the riverbank where he could see more clearly. It took him a few moments before he could make out exactly what the things in the car were.

Possums. Six of them. In his new car.

"Mate, this is ridiculous!" he whispered. "They're only possums!"

"That's all very well, mate," said Bren. "But this bunch of possums managed to start the engine, right?"

Bret nodded as the Land Cruiser backed away from the edge of the river, all the way back toward the entrance to the boat-ramp car park.

"They're stealing it!" wailed Bret.

Engine revving and tires spinning wildly on the gravel, the big car twirled expertly in a smoking figure eight. Then the possums straightened it out, the rear tires screaming in a cloud of burning rubber and hot tar. With a roar the brake was released and the Land Cruiser shot toward the river.

"I don't think they're stealing it, mate!" said Bren as the car hurtled toward them gathering speed with every meter. "I reckon they're crashing it!"

Three tons of Japanese metal soared out over Bret and Bren's heads at eighty kilometers an hour. At the last possible moment six possums leaped from the side windows and landed on the thick grass of the bank where they rolled acrobatically to safety. The big car plunged nose first into the river with an almighty splash. There was a quiet moment when the only sound was Bret moaning, before the car tilted its rear end toward the sky and sank, the engine dying in a bubbling roar of steam and water.

Bren and Bret stood openmouthed as the river closed over the Land Cruiser. From above and behind them came an odd hacking sound. What now, thought Bret? He turned slowly, his shoulders slumped, a beaten man.

Six possums sat in a line on the riverbank rocking back and forth. One of them held a discarded shake container.

If Bret hadn't known better, he'd have sworn they were laughing.

Chapter 17

Behind The Pig in a Poke, The Brain quickly stripped off his reporter disguise. Off came the suit, the hat, the beard, the padded stomach, and the ministilts that had been strapped to his shins. He picked impatiently at shreds of latex that clung stubbornly to his face. Finished at last, he wadded the disguise into a ball and stowed it inside one of Iggy's dumpsters.

"Let's go," he said, glancing around the side of The Pig. "Come, Sheldon, time is of the essence! Events are unfolding with extreme rapidity and I sense that we must act, and act quickly! Observe!"

He pointed across the road to a small paddock where Mr. Burgess kept his old horse, Smudger. Smudger was the oldest horse Sheldon had ever seen and he had been quietly munching grass in that paddock for as long as Sheldon could remember. Right now Smudger was hunched down in the long grass inching forward toward a bush where a sparrow sat on a branch. Smudger kept his head down, moving as purposefully and gracefully as a leopard. A few meters from the bush, Smudger sprang powerfully into the air and grabbed the sparrow between his yellowed teeth. He shook the bird violently and swallowed it in one savage movement.

"Good grief!" yelped Sheldon. "What was *that*?"

"You see?" said The Brain. "There's not a moment to lose! I was afraid that it would accelerate!"

He turned and strode purposefully up the hill. Sheldon looked disbelievingly at Smudger, now standing calmly in the paddock chewing slowly, a lone feather clinging to his upper lip the only clue as to what had just happened. Sheldon shook his head and jogged after The Brain.

"What will accelerate? Where are we going?" puffed Sheldon as they rounded the bend at the crest of the rise that led away from The Pig.

"Shhsshh!" hissed The Brain, pointing up ahead. Sheldon followed his finger. About fifty meters ahead of them, Miss Fleming, moving quickly, turned into a side road. The Brain pressed Sheldon back against the bushes until she'd passed from sight.

"We're following *Fleming*?" Sheldon whispered frantically. "Are you nuts? Have you gone *completely* mad? She'll kill us if she sees us!"

"Let us see, Sheldon, let us see. If my theories are correct, I think Miss Fleming is an important player in our little affair."

"And if they're not correct...your theories, I mean? Where does that leave us then?"

The Brain waved aside Sheldon's worries with a

casual flick of his bony wrist and moved smoothly in the direction Fleming had taken. Muttering mutinously under his breath, Sheldon followed.

"What's so wrong with Fleming, anyway?" Sheldon asked as they hurried toward her house. "I mean, I know I think she's horrible and probably some sort of mutant space-creature or something, but that's all a load of rubbish, really. Isn't it?"

"I ran Fleming's name and image through a few of my gizmos—my Name Recognition Data Interface Module and my new Facial Recognition software."

"And?"

"And nothing, Sheldon. There is no record of Fleming on any criminal database and no mention of her being involved in anything illegal anywhere in the world."

The Brain paused and looked very pleased with himself.

"So why are we following her, if she hasn't done anything?" said Sheldon, puzzled.

The Brain held up a finger.

"I didn't say she hadn't *done* anything; I said her name didn't come up on any criminal list. The two things are quite separate. Besides, I have known there was something not right about Fleming ever since I laid eyes on her. However, I think I may have miscalculated just how much was not right about her. I'm not going to make that mistake again. Mark my words, Sheldon, she's up to her nasty little eyeballs in this caper and it's our job to find out exactly how!"

Two minutes later the pair were hunched uncomfortably behind an overgrown azalea bush at the side of

Fleming's house. It looked like any regular house, thought Sheldon: windows, doors, brick, and wood, all that kind of thing. There were frilled curtains on the windows and, from what he could glimpse inside, perfectly normal-looking furniture and house stuff.

But this *was* Fleming's house, he reminded himself, and, as such, must contain a torture laboratory, an alien-egg nest, a stainless-steel-and-leather command post, or some other spooky and mysterious secret, surely? Yes, it all *looked* normal on the outside, but Sheldon would've bet there was a shark pit lurking under the flowerbeds and a dungeon housed below the garden shed.

The Brain left the azalea bush and sidled up to the side of the house. He ducked down underneath a small side window.

"What are you doing?" Sheldon hissed, his eyes wide with fear.

The Brain signaled for him to come closer. Sheldon shook his head. Uh-uh, no way. The Brain signaled again, more urgently. Shooting a look of pure hatred at The Brain, Sheldon shuffled forward, hardly daring to breathe. When he took on this sidekick job he knew it might involve making sacrifices. Sheldon just hoped it wouldn't turn out to be human sacrifice.

Sheldon reached the side of the house and rested against the white wall, his heart jackhammering inside his chest.

"Good of you to join me," said The Brain. "Now, if you have quite finished, we can proceed."

He pointed toward the window.

"Miss Fleming's bedroom," he whispered.

"Oh no, no, no, no, no, no, no!" Sheldon whispered back. "This is getting *weird*. We don't want to be peeking in at Fleming's window, do we? She might be in her knickers or something, or *worse*. I'm gonna hurl for sure if she's, like, eating a child, or wrapping some dude up in some nasty gooey egg-thing. I'll probably hurl even if she's just standing there in her knickers."

The Brain made a *tchah* sound and regally waved away Sheldon's objections.

They raised their eyes slowly to the window level and, through a chink in the blind, looked right into Fleming's bedroom.

Into the belly of the beast, thought Sheldon gloomily.

He couldn't see much. The Brain's head kept getting in the way and Sheldon was handicapped by cowardice. Sheldon expected to feel Fleming's hand on his shoulder at any moment. After a second or two his eyes adjusted focus and he could see what was happening inside Fleming's bedroom.

It was, as Sheldon had predicted, horrible. More horrible than even just imagining it.

She was in her knickers.

"Oh, man!" Sheldon groaned, his legs wobbling. "That's, like…um, jeez, dude!"

The Brain nudged him in the ribs.

"Pull yourself together, Sheldon," he whispered. "Look."

Sheldon choked back the bile rising in his throat and forced his reluctant eyes to return to the vision of Fleming in her underpants. There she stood, undressed and wrinkled and horrid. Her knickers were enormous and her bra looked like a piece of military equipment. Just as Sheldon thought things couldn't possibly get any worse, Fleming raised her hair up and lifted it clean off her head to reveal a gleaming pink pate. She was completely bald and the hair loss did nothing to improve her appearance. Fleming put the wig down on a shelf inside her wardrobe and began to unhook her bra.

"C'mon," Sheldon squeaked, clutching frantically at The Brain's sleeve. "Enough is enough. I'm begging you. There are some things that simply *aren't meant to be seen*. Ever! Fleming in the nude is one of them, perhaps the biggest one of all."

The Brain hadn't moved.

"Look," he said simply.

Reluctantly, very reluctantly, Sheldon turned to look and immediately wished he hadn't. What he saw, he was certain, would stay with him until the day he died, the image burned indelibly onto the hard drive of his cerebral cortex.

Fleming unhooked her bra and lifted it off...along with her breasts and stomach, which all came off in one quivering, rubbery lump. Sheldon groaned, wobbled, and closed his eyes tight. The Brain nudged him.

"It's all right, old bean. It's latex," he said. "Fleming is wearing a latex woman-suit."

"A...*what*? A *woman-suit*? Did I hear you right? What the hell is a woman-suit?"

Sheldon looked again. In the middle of her bedroom, bald, completely nude, and extremely wrinkled, Miss Fleming stood just as she came into the world.

She was a man.

Chapter 18

Sheldon! Sheldon! Shel-don!" Sheldon opened his eyes to see The Brain looming over him, a concerned look on his face.

"Ah, there you are, old thing. Got quite worried about you for a moment. Do you often faint?"

"Only when I see stuff like *that*," said Sheldon, lifting himself up on one elbow and pointing up at Fleming's window. "What the hell was *that* all about?"

He stopped suddenly, panicked once more.

"She, it, I mean he's not on to us is she, I mean he?"

The Brain shook his head.

"Fleming, if that is his name, (which I strongly doubt), is at this moment taking a shower. I calculate that wearing that latex disguise would raise his body temperature by a factor of three at least, and would require regular showering to regulate. We have ample time to look around."

"Look around? You don't mean we're going in there? Well, you can forget that for a start. There's absolutely no way I'm going in that house!"

Inside Fleming's house it was quiet, apart from the distant hiss of a shower.

"I'm only staying for a few minutes," Sheldon squeaked. "Then I'm gone, sidekick or no sidekick."

"A few minutes should be sufficient," said The Brain, peering under books and sliding open drawers.

"This isn't good. What if Snook gets wind of this? The McGlones would be a one-family crime wave in Farrago!"

"Please relax, Sheldon, there's a good fellow," said The Brain. He could have been taking a stroll around the deck of a luxury cruise liner, his attitude was so breezy. "Even if Fleming does discover us, he will not call the police. After all, it doesn't look good, does it...all that pretense? I imagine that, armed with our knowledge of her real status, 'Miss' Fleming would be mere putty in our hands."

Something flickered at the back of Sheldon's mind. Something The Brain said had triggered a memory.

"You knew!" he gasped. "That was how you controlled her back on your first day at school."

"Correct, my dear Sheldon. I was aware that Fleming was not all she claimed to be. The evidence was instantly clear to anyone with eyes. Her large hands, her height, the curious rubbery texture of her skin, the tone of her voice. All pointing in one direction: masculinity. I merely made the logical deduction and informed her. I mentioned that her secret was safe with me as long as *I* remained safe whilst in Farrago Bay."

The Brain inspected the contents of a decorative box on a shelf.

"The question now is: *why* is Fleming dressing as a woman and *why* is he interested in the Manly murder?"

"Is she...he?" said Sheldon. "Interested in the Manly murder, I mean?"

"I would say so," said The Brain, opening the door to a long wooden cupboard in a corner of Fleming's living room. "Wouldn't you?"

Sheldon peered inside.

The cupboard was lined with cork tile, almost every square centimeter of which had been covered with photos, drawings, press clippings, graphs, internet printouts—all relating in one way or another to Biff Manly's murder. With a shock, Sheldon saw two glossy photographs of himself and The Brain, apparently taken by a camera with a high-powered zoom lens. Leaning closer, Sheldon saw they had been shot through the window of his house the night The Brain and he became a team. Scrawled in red crayon on the photo was a note that said "Important?" and an arrow that pointed to Sheldon. There were more photos of The Brain in a stack at the rear of the cupboard.

"Man, this is spooky. We should go, like now."

"I'm inclined to agree, my good fellow," said The Brain. "Although possibly not for the same reason you outlined. I notice that the shower has ceased."

He was right. Fleming had finished in the shower. The Brain slid across the room to the bedroom door and put one of his round eyes to the crack.

"Tell me what you see, Sheldon," he said, and pulled Sheldon toward the door.

"We've got to get out of here!"

"Please," said The Brain. "Tell me what you see."

Reluctantly Sheldon put his eye to the door. The bedroom looked normal enough. A large bed, a wardrobe, a bedside table. Next to the bed was a large cardboard box containing hundreds of tubes of toothpaste.

"OK," said Sheldon, "I've seen it. Can we go now?"

"You are seeing, Sheldon, but you are not observing. What can you deduce from what you have seen?"

"It's just a room," said Sheldon.

"And the toothpaste? You do not consider that to be important?"

Before Sheldon could answer the door to the bathroom opened and Fleming stepped into the bedroom. Nude.

Quicker than you could say "brown trousers," Sheldon and The Brain sprinted across the shag pile and dived out the half-open window. Sheldon hunkered down into the dirt, ignoring the mass of ants gnawing at his ear. If it was a choice between ants in his ear canal and Fleming on the warpath, Sheldon decided he'd opt for the insects every time.

A few moments passed during which nothing much happened. Sheldon breathed through his nose and spat out a couple of ants. Then the Brain motioned to Sheldon and the two slipped away from the house into the relative safety of the azalea bushes. A few minutes later they were walking back toward The Pig, Sheldon happy to put Fleming's Cross-Dressing House of Weirdness behind him. He needed a resuscitating chocolate-macadamia-nut-banana smoothie and, hopefully, some answers to the cloud of questions swirling around inside his head.

Chapter 19

Sheldon clutched the smoothie the way a drowning man clutches a life preserver. He slurped about half of it down in one quick action. After what he'd just witnessed—and he was having difficulty really believing that he had actually seen the things he'd just seen—he needed, required, *demanded* something to take his mind off it. He took a long pull on the straw. He was shivering and finding it hard to speak. The Brain told him it was a form of Posttraumatic Stress Disorder, the same thing that soldiers got after really horrible experiences during wartime. Sheldon didn't know what the soldiers were moaning about; he'd like to see anyone cope after going through the experience he'd just been through.

Sheldon held the smoothie and waited for The Brain to make some sense of what they'd seen.

The Pig in a Poke was almost deserted now, the press conference long over and the reporters gone to file their reports. Horrocks and the shady blond man had, presumably, crawled back under a nearby stone.

Snook had left, too, no doubt to watch himself on the lunchtime news.

Iggy and a couple of his regulars leaned on the counter discussing something of international importance, or possibly the chances of rain later in the afternoon.

Sheldon was so shaken by the adventure at Fleming's lair that he hardly registered the fact that Fergus Feebly and his mob sat in a nearby booth. After recent events, Feebly had moved a long way down the table of Things To Be Worried About.

The Brain stirred his tea thoughtfully and gazed out of the window. He looked as though he was waiting for something. The daily life of Farrago Bay carried on. Shoppers shopped. Tourists touristed. Surfers cycled past carrying boards to the beach. A line of slow-moving cars drove past looking for parking spaces or simply passing through. A long black car detached itself from the rest and slid to a halt outside The Pig. The Brain cast a cool glance in its direction, turned back to face Sheldon, and replaced his cup on the table.

"Tip-top tea," he said. "For these parts."

"Never mind the tea, man! What about all that crazy stuff back there? What are we going to *do*?"

"Toothpaste," said The Brain.

"What do you mean, toothpaste? All that...that man/woman stuff and you're thinking about toothpaste?"

The Brain flicked another glance at the long black car before replying.

"You no doubt observed that Fleming had a large

box of toothpaste in his bedroom? I consider the toothpaste to be of the utmost significance in this case, Sheldon. It has started me on a train of thought and that train is now careening down a track, fixed firmly upon its destination."

The Brain held up a finger to halt a question from Sheldon, who was not convinced of the importance of toothpaste in the case.

"The toothpaste holds the key to an important connection in this case. It is one thing to order a few extra tubes of toothpaste but quite another to have it delivered in batches of five hundred. It is an important pointer to the true nature of this mystery! Why would Fleming have so much toothpaste?"

Personally, Sheldon still thought it was a bit of a stretch to connect the toothpaste to Biff's murder, but then The Brain was the expert here, wasn't he? Unless he really was from Mooloolaba, in which case he was just flying a kite and Sheldon would really be better off tucked up in front of a computer game. There were times when he thought he'd rather not be part of all this. This was one of those times. Still, there was Sean to think about. If Sheldon and The Brain didn't manage to prove the truth about all this, then Sean was going to spend the rest of his life in a cell. So Sheldon listened to what The Brain was saying.

"There is also the small matter of the chief witness against your brother being a convicted felon. It is curiously *fortunate*, is it not, that Horrocks should be the only witness? Not to mention the discovery of Sean's hairs under Manly's fingernails after Miss Madison had made her examination. She does not strike me as being a person who would miss something as obvious as that."

"You mean they were planted there?" said Sheldon. "By whom? Snook?"

The Brain shook his head.

"Of course not. Sergeant Snook has neither the imagination nor the criminality to even think of such a thing. Planting DNA evidence requires skill. Even if Snook had wanted to I'm sure he would have failed. Besides, what would he have to gain?"

"He'd get Sean convicted."

"Correct, but he would lose the affections of your mother—granted, that may already have happened— but, more importantly, Snook is someone who, I believe, tries to play fair. No, the person who planted that evidence is of an altogether different type. And, if I'm not mistaken, our paths will cross before too long, if they haven't already. There is something about Miss Fleming that is oddly familiar."

The Brain looked around, an anxious expression suddenly crossing his pale face.

"What?" Sheldon hissed, his nerves jangling, adrenaline levels shooting back up the scale. "Is it Fleming?"

"The toilet," said The Brain. "Could you point me in the right direction? That tea's gone straight to my plumbing."

Sheldon sank back into the booth, pointing to the rest rooms. Iggy walked over and asked if Sheldon needed a top-up. It wasn't every day that you see your teacher turn from an alien woman-beast into a bloke in front of your eyes, so Sheldon gave him the nod and requested extra chocolate sauce. Just for the energy levels.

As Iggy waddled back behind the counter, Sheldon noticed Feebly slip out of the booth and head toward the toilet. Sheldon didn't like the look of that one little bit. Sheldon had seen The Brain subdue Feebly before, true, but who was to say he'd be able to do it again? There was something about today that felt like trouble.

As if they didn't have enough to deal with with.

Sheldon glanced down at his watch. Another minute and he'd have to go help The Brain with Feebly. Sheldon knew he'd probably get dunked headfirst, just like last year when he made the mistake of arriving in the school toilets at the same time as Feebly.

The deadline passed and Sheldon hoisted himself, reluctantly, out of the booth. With heavy tread, he walked slowly toward the rest room. He would normally have been more than a little nervous pushing open the toilet door of The Pig, given Iggy's questionable cleanliness record. Now, he was scared. He took a deep breath and barged in.

It was empty.

There was no one there. A complete absence of Feebly, The Brain, of anyone. The only clue that humans had recently been here (besides the usual cat-blinding stench and the graffiti) was the ragged curtain hanging in the open window, gently moving back and forth in the breeze.

Sheldon got to the window just in time to see the long black car purr away, fast, from the parking lot.

Through the rear window Sheldon could see the blond man driving, Horrocks in the passenger seat. Horrocks was turned to the rear of the car, mouthing something as if talking to someone out of sight, someone pushed to the floor, or locked in the boot perhaps. Sheldon couldn't see The Brain, or Feebly for that matter, but it didn't take a genius to work out what had happened.

The Brain had been kidnapped. So, it seemed, had Feebly. Sheldon could feel in his guts that he was right about this.

Action would be required.

Chapter 20

This had to be the low point of the entire thing, Sheldon thought gloomily. Literally in the toilet. Alone. Solo. Solitary. The Brain gone. Sheldon could have said he was Brainless, *har har har,* if he'd felt much like laughing. Which he didn't.

Sidekicks weren't *supposed* to be alone were they? That was the whole *point* of sidekicks; they should always be found at the side of the detective asking dumb questions and occasionally helping, while the detective wrapped things up nice and neatly at the end. Sheldon was confident he could manage the dumb questions bit, no problem at all, piece of cake; he had after all been practicing *that* aspect of the job most of his life. He reckoned he could even stumble accidentally on an important piece of information from time to time if pushed, but *this* situation, dealing with things by himself, making actual meaningful decisions, was most certainly not in the job description.

This was serious stuff. Kidnapping was kidnapping and, for all Sheldon knew, Horrocks and that creepy blond guy were busy chopping The Brain (and Feebly) into handy bite-sized chunks right at that moment. It was definitely time for action.

Sheldon rushed back into the cafe.

"Get the police! That bloke from Dent-O has kidnapped The Brain and Feebly and has taken them off in a long black car!"

The reaction was distinctly underwhelming.

Iggy didn't so much as stir from his stool by the cash register. He looked up sleepily.

"Wha'?"

"Kid says someone's been kidded or something," said one of the coffee-addled regulars sitting at the counter.

"Not kidded," squealed Sheldon. *"Kidnapped!"*

Without their trusted leader, Feebly's crew reminded Sheldon of a bunch of particularly indecisive jellyfish. They looked back and forth between him and Iggy and alternated uncertainly between sniggers and sneers.

Sheldon decided action would speak louder than words. He walked to the counter and grabbed the phone purposefully from behind the register. Ignoring Iggy's yabberings about the phone being only for staff use, Sheldon jabbed in the number for the police station.

"Tell Sergeant Snook to get over to The Pig in a Poke!" he yelled in an authoritative voice as soon as his call was answered.

Unfortunately he'd dialed EZ-Video on Beach Road by mistake, and had to start again after dealing with a very confused Mrs. Poom, the elderly owner.

Sheldon dialed again with as much dignity as he could muster.

"Get over to The Pig in a Poke right away!" he yelled, having gotten the number right this time. "There's been a kidnapping!"

To be fair to the bobbies, Sheldon had to admit, they didn't waste much time arriving. Five minutes after making the call, Sheldon was being quizzed by Snook in one of the booths. Ken and Phil stood to one side looking extremely intelligent and professional (which just goes to show what you can learn by watching cop shows on TV). Gary must have been out on sleeping duty.

The problem was that now that the police had arrived, Sheldon was having difficulty convincing Snook he was serious. Sheldon was, after all, the brother of a murder suspect, and the friend of Farrago Bay's biggest interfering busybody who, worse still, had allowed his pet croc to treat Snook like a chew toy.

This wasn't going to be an easy sell.

"Let me get this straight," said Snook, sneering theatrically and leaning against the side of a booth. "Your friend, the crocodile lover, was kidnapped by the managing director of the biggest factory in the Bay and driven off in a black car?"

"Don't forget Feebly," Ken added helpfully.

"Oh, and Mr. Feebly too, that's right. Thanks, Ken," said Snook. He sighed and ran his hand over his hair. Probably checking to be sure all six of them were still there, thought Sheldon.

Snook shouted over to Iggy and the regulars.

"Any of you blokes see Mr. Horrocks creeping about with a baseball bat and carting off spotty youths?"

There was general head shaking and lip pursing

from the yokels, which indicated that, now that they thought about it, no they hadn't.

"No," said Snook, turning back to Sheldon. "Didn't think so. Look, McGlone, there's not a scrap of evidence to suggest that Mr. Horrocks has got anything to do with your two pals scarpering through the toilet window. Probably trying to get out of paying, if I know anything about young people. Or," he added, "they may just have been anxious to get as far from any spare McGlones as *I* would be. Count yourself lucky we don't charge you with wasting police time."

"Yeah!" said Phil, hoisting up his gun belt and glowering at Sheldon. He pointed a podgy finger.

Snook stood upright, adjusted his own belt, put on his hat, and swaggered out of The Pig, taking care to slowly replace his new mirrored sunglasses.

Sheldon stood up and shouted at Snook's back.

"I should have known you'd do nothing! Well, I'm going to rescue The Brain myself!"

Snook carried on walking and Sheldon sat down.

It was one thing to say he was going to rescue The Brain, but it was quite another to actually do it. Where to start? Sheldon's head slumped toward the Formica tabletop and he let out a long slow groan. What was he *doing*? He'd never be able to think of anything useful!

And just like that, the answer came to him.

Dent-O.

Dent-O was involved in this somehow. Someone was trying to pin the blame on Sean for Biff's murder, and that person was Horrocks. It was Horrocks who had said he'd seen Sean kill Biff. It was Horrocks who had paid for the second autopsy to discover the DNA evidence. It was Horrocks had driven off just after The Brain (and Feebly) had disappeared. Horrocks, Horrocks, Horrocks.

Sheldon didn't know how or why, or where Fleming came into it (although maybe that was why The Brain had been banging on about all that toothpaste in her bedroom), or how Mavis had ended up as a Yorkshire terrier, or any of the rest of that stuff, but he knew that Horrocks was, for all intents and purposes, Mr. Dent-O in these parts. More to the point, Sheldon couldn't stand him and would like nothing better than to wipe that big fat smooth grin off that big fat smooth face of his. That was assuming Horrocks didn't get away with it. And Sheldon had seen enough to know that was likely. Evil factory owners always got their come-uppance in the end, didn't they?

Energized, Sheldon got to his feet. It was time to stand up and be counted.

Next stop Dent-O.

Chapter 21

Situation Code Red with cherries on top: check. Butterflies in stomach: check. About a klick out from the target perimeter. Sheldon didn't know how far a klick was, but he reckoned this looked about right. He didn't even know why he was using words like "perimeter," or "klick," or "check," but it seemed to help.

He crept through the undergrowth toward the Dent-O factory with extreme caution, green camouflage on his face applied using some old party face paints found at the bottom of a kitchen drawer at home. A woolen beanie was pulled down close to his eyes. This, along with a pair of green jeans and an old army-style jacket, made up his uniform. Call him stupid, thought Sheldon, but only by pretending he was playing soldiers could he summon the courage to do this on his own.

Deep in the rainforest remnants that clung to the hillside around the Dent-O factory, three kilometers out of Farrago Bay, strange shadows rippled and loomed, sending little spurts of adrenaline down into Sheldon's already wobbly legs. Odd rustlings from here and there in the bush sounded to Sheldon like a platoon of brown snakes were out on an evening stroll. Sheldon hated the forest but he'd had no choice. He hadn't been able to risk using the main road up to the factory in case Dent-O had posted guards on all approaches or booby-trapped the road or something.

Which meant here he was, deep in the bush, dressed like someone from a low-budget war movie, sneaking up on a toothpaste factory armed with only an adjustable spanner (Sheldon had picked it up from the garage when he set out, largely because it seemed stupid to go up there with nothing) and a mobile phone (his mother's, snaffled in case things really started going south).

Sheldon didn't have any clear plans about exactly what he'd do once he reached the Dent-O factory; he just hoped that he got through it in one piece.

It was a relief when the factory came into view: at least he hadn't gotten lost. Sheldon stopped. It was, strangely, the first time he'd seen the Dent-O factory. It was built on a road he had no reason to use and, since he didn't make a habit of blundering blindly through snake-infested rainforest, he had certainly never stumbled across it from the bush before.

It didn't look like much.

The Dent-O factory was simply a long, dusty, cement-block building with a corrugated-tin roof. Sticking out here and there were various nondescript out-buildings that looked as though they had been bolted on when more space was needed. All that separated

Sheldon from the factory was a single wire fence. The place was deserted and Sheldon got the clear idea he could probably walk in without attracting so much as a sideways glance from a cane toad. Still, better not take any unnecessary chances. He would walk around the fence to check for security staff. Piece of cake.

Something nudged him hard in the back. Leaping like a scalded ferret, he whirled round and came face to face with a large crocodile, its jaws inches from his stomach.

It was a measure of how things had changed in Sheldon's world that he didn't drop stone dead on the spot. Instead, he gave a sigh of relief at the sight of Mavis. She was holding a big stick in her mouth and wagging her tail, which, Sheldon fervently prayed, meant she was still in Yorkshire terrier mode.

Still, he could do without the distraction of Mavis right now. He'd have to get rid of her.

"Mavis!" he whispered. "Shoo!"

Mavis gave no sign of shooing. If anything, she wagged her tail more vigorously. At least, thought Sheldon, it was proof that she did still think she was a dog, which was infinitely preferable to her thinking she was a crocodile. Sheldon picked the stick out from between her jaws, taking care not to get any part of his body in range of her teeth, and, with some effort, threw it into the bush. Mavis gave a bark of joy and blundered happily after it disturbing an enormous flock of lorikeets that flew up into the air screeching loudly.

So much for the sneaky approach.

When Mavis got back with her stick, Sheldon did

his best to suggest to her, using sign language and facial expressions, that they should tone it down a bit and keep quiet while he sneaked into the factory. But he couldn't be sure she followed much of it.

With a resigned shrug he set off up the hill toward the Dent-O fence, leading Mavis by throwing the stick every now and again. Sheldon knew that approaching the factory accompanied by a five-meter crocodile would probably tip them off he was coming, but he thought he'd cross that bridge when he came to it. He was the sidekick, remember? He wasn't supposed to have a Big Plan tucked away up his sleeve somewhere. Which was just as well, as Sheldon had nothing that remotely resembled a Plan, big or small, tucked anywhere. The best he could come up with was to go with the flow and hope for the best. It didn't sound convincing, even to Sheldon.

By the time he reached the fence, Mavis had calmed down somewhat. Like an overgrown puppy, she lay on her back and rubbed against the ground, growling softly at the stick. Sheldon remembered what had happened to Snook and smiled.

OK, what next?

Sheldon took hold of the fence, half-expecting it to be electrified. Images of himself being fried to a blackened crisp sprang into his mind, but the fence was safe.

"Oh well," he muttered to himself. "Here goes nothing." He began to climb. He had managed about a meter when Mavis tugged at his foot. Sheldon shook it but she wouldn't let go. With an exasperated sigh he dropped to the ground. Mavis was wagging her tail expectantly and looking meaningfully at the stick. There was no mistaking what she wanted. Sheldon shook his head, picked up the stick, and threw it as far down the line of the fence as he could. Throwing had never been his strong point, especially with the size and weight of stick that Mavis preferred. The stick curved in the air, hit the top strand of wire, and toppled into the Dent-O factory on the other side of the fence. Mavis looked at her beloved stick and back at Sheldon.

"Oops, sorry, Mavis," he whispered.

Mavis turned and crashed straight through the fence, joyfully grabbing her stick. Sheldon almost whooped with delight.

They were in!

As Sheldon trotted quickly up to the side of the nearest building, he signaled for Mavis to follow him. Based on how she'd handled the fence, a tame crocodile might come in handy after all. He fumbled in his jacket for the packet of sweets he'd brought for rations, and held one out to Mavis. She opened her jaws and Sheldon popped one inside. He walked along the side of the factory toward the front entrance, Mavis following, quietly chewing mints.

At the corner of the building, Sheldon was able to get an idea of where he was in the Dent-O complex. The front entrance of the factory lay dead ahead, the office car park in front of it empty in the blazing sun. About fifty meters away, a red-roofed security hut stood at an opening in the fence. A guard snoozed inside, his feet propped up on a counter. Sheldon could see his blue-clad legs through the window, a yellow stripe running the length of them.

From the look of the guard's relaxed pose, not to mention the fact that he was alone, it didn't look like it was much of a high-security operation. Surely, if Horrocks was the evil mastermind, there'd be a bit more show than all this? Maybe The Brain had been barking up the wrong tree after all. Perhaps Dent-O was a perfectly ordinary toothpaste factory and not the hub of an evil criminal empire.

Sheldon shook himself. All this was getting him nowhere. The Brain was somewhere, that was certain, and Dent-O was the only possible lead he had. It was Dent-O or nothing.

"C'mon, Sheldon," he muttered. "Think!"

Before anything intelligent popped into Sheldon's head, a glint of sun reflected on something on the far side of the car park and caught his eye. Squinting, Sheldon saw the long black car he'd last seen speeding away from The Pig. It was tucked up tight against a narrow side door.

A buzz of excitement shot through Sheldon's central nervous system. If the car was there, there was at least a chance that The Brain was there too.

The big question was, where?

Now that he thought about it, there was something funny about the car. Why would Horrocks, the managing director of Dent-O, park his car in such an out-of-the-way spot *and* so close to a sneaky little side entrance? It could only mean one thing: Horrocks and the creepy blond man had parked there to shovel The Brain and Feebly inside Dent-O without the security guard knowing about it.

Sheldon glanced toward the security hut. The guard

had woken up and was stretching. While the guard was asleep Sheldon had had a clear run toward the door by Horrocks's car. Now that the guard was awake, the odds had shifted.

Sheldon looked around for inspiration. His eye fell on Mavis and, in an instant, Sheldon knew what to do. He picked up her stick. It wasn't much of a plan but it would have to do.

Sheldon drew back both arms and aimed for a spot about ten meters beyond the security hut. As soon as the stick was in the air Sheldon knew the throw hadn't been good enough. With a sort of horrifying inevitability, the stick bounced on the roof of the hut with a dull clang and dropped to the ground. The guard sat up as if his trousers were on fire. He opened the door and looked around, puzzled. His eye caught the stick lying on the ground and he bent down and picked it up.

Sheldon was close enough to see the shock of disbelief on the guard's face as he realized that nine-hundred kilos of crocodile nightmare was barreling toward him out of nowhere.

With a high-pitched yelp, the guard jumped back inside and hurled himself, quivering, under his desk three seconds before Mavis hit the security hut like a runaway train. With a sickening crunch, the flimsy hut disintegrated in an explosion of splintered wood and twisted corrugated metal.

Sheldon closed his eyes, then opened them as the dust cleared to reveal Mavis, coated in a thin layer of debris, standing in the center of what had been the hut. The dust gave her a ghostly, otherworldly air. Sheldon wouldn't have believed it possible, but Mavis looked even scarier than usual. From the dazed viewpoint of the security guard she must have looked like some creature from the lower depths of hell. Surrounded by more sticks than she could chase in a lifetime, Mavis gave a howl of delight. The security guard screamed and sprinted down Farrago Road, Mavis's original stick still clutched in his hand.

Sheldon seized his chance and ran across the car park straight toward the black car. He glanced back toward the rubble of the security hut and saw Mavis chasing the security guard.

The guard's in for an interesting afternoon, thought Sheldon.

Sheldon reached the door, said a small prayer, and stepped inside.

Chapter 22

Armed only with a size-ten spanner and as many crossed fingers as he could manage, Sheldon looked around. If he'd been expecting the volcano lair of an evil mastermind, he was disappointed.

The door opened onto a small corridor with a few bits of ratty office furniture, some discarded cardboard, and a potted plant that had seen better days. A nasty green carpet had some marks on it that might, to a really suspicious person whose nerves were jangling like wind chimes in a hurricane (like Sheldon, for example), have looked as though someone or something had recently been dragged along it. Sheldon took a lingering look at the door he'd just come in through. It would be so easy to back out now.

He didn't. It was funny, but whenever Sheldon read a book or watched a movie in which one of the characters went into a dangerous situation, he always thought, "Why don't you just run? It's obvious you're going to get it if you go in there." Yet here he was, in exactly that situation, doing just that.

Sheldon tiptoed his way along the corridor past deserted Dent-O offices, computer standby lights blinking in the darkened rooms. He arrived at a long internal window overlooking the main part of the Dent-O operation. It looked just as Sheldon would have imagined a toothpaste factory would look: lots of pipes, machinery, and wiring, all very clean, all in good order. It was a little discouraging. The fact that Dent-O looked like a real toothpaste factory might have been evidence that this was precisely what it was: a real toothpaste factory. Which, Sheldon thought, made it less likely that he was on the right track.

More and more convinced that he was indeed barking up the wrong tree, Sheldon passed through a door into the factory and started to explore. His frustration grew stronger with every passing minute. There was no indication that The Brain, Fergus Feebly, or even Horrocks had even visited the place.

Sheldon peered under machines, rummaged around in the back of storage spaces, felt behind drink dispensers, and discovered nothing. This was all completely useless. He was getting nowhere. He was also conscious of the fact that, if Dent-O turned out to be a completely innocent toothpaste factory, Sheldon would now be the lawbreaker as far as Snook was concerned. Being charged with breaking and entering wouldn't go down very well with his mother either, thought Sheldon gloomily. He'd give it a couple more minutes and then try to think of another great plan—hopefully one that didn't involve extreme personal danger.

The next moment, extreme personal danger seemed

much more likely. Sheldon heard a strangely familiar noise. He hit the floor like a sack of potatoes and rolled under a nearby machine. The smell of mint was almost overpowering. His eyes watered—the effects of the chemicals or naked fear? He couldn't tell.

The sound of footsteps. A pair of feet clopped into view. Sheldon wedged himself tighter into the crawl-space below the mint machine and tried his very best to disappear. He let his breath out in long, slow, shallow bursts. It was going to be OK. The footsteps passed him, less than two meters away. Whoever it was didn't know Sheldon was there. All he had to do was keep very, very quiet.

It was then that Sheldon farted.

Parp.

Only a small one, hardly a squeak, but enough to stop the feet moving. Sheldon clenched his buttocks, held his breath, and waited.

Someone sniffed, the sound echoing in the empty factory. Fear shot through Sheldon. The sniffer bent down far enough to reveal a hand holding a large, extremely nasty-looking semiautomatic weapon. Sheldon's guts turned to custard.

Time seemed to stand still until, amazingly, unbelievably, the feet moved on and clanked away. Sheldon relaxed carefully, taking care not to accidentally let out another squeak. He was more scared than ever, and not just because there was a creepy person inside Dent-O clutching a large gun. There were two very significant things he'd noticed about the newcomer. First, it was wearing a dress. Secondly, he'd recognize that sniff anywhere.

It was his worst nightmare come true: Fleming with a gun.

What *was* Fleming doing here? And armed, to boot? Sheldon cautiously rolled out from under the crawl-space and stood up. Ahead of him, Fleming turned to the left. As quietly as possible, Sheldon crept after him.

As Sheldon reached the corner of the building he heard a familiar voice.

"Miss Fleming, I've been wondering when you would arrive," the voice said. "Can I say how divine you are looking this evening? The gun adds a distinctly masculine touch to your ensemble."

The Brain! He was still alive—and still giving Fleming a hard time. Sheldon could have danced. Instead he contented himself with the knowledge that he'd been right about coming to Dent-O. Maybe he was becoming a detective after all!

"Shut up!" shouted Fleming. There was a sharp thwack and The Brain grunted in pain. He made a spitting sound.

"A tooth," said The Brain. "I shall be sure to remember that when the time comes to deal with you, Miss Fleming...or should I call you *Mr.* Fleming?"

Another voice cut in, sobbing. "Miss Fleming," whined Feebly. "It was all his fault! That weird Pommie, I always knew he was trouble!"

"Be quiet, Feebly, you irritating yokel," snapped Fleming.

Feebly didn't seem to have heard. He wailed like a

police siren, begging Fleming to shoot The Brain and to leave him alone.

"Stay quiet, old boy," The Brain said quietly and urgently to Feebly.

"Oh, shut up!" screamed Feebly. "What do you know, you big-headed freak? It's all your fault I'm here in the first place. If it wasn't for you, none of this would ever have happened and now we're stuck here with all these guns and everything's gone wrong and it's all your fault and—"

There was a sudden burst of gunfire and Feebly stopped talking. Sheldon held his breath, frozen in horror. Had Fleming shot Feebly? This whole thing was getting unbearable. Then, to Sheldon's relief, Feebly whimpered, and Sheldon realized that Fleming had simply fired a few warning shots into the roof.

Sheldon spotted an iron ladder. At the roof, it met a gangway that ran all the way around the main factory. From up there, Sheldon would have a better view of the situation. What he'd do with that view when he got up there was another matter, but Sheldon was a firm believer in doing one thing at a time.

Showing astonishing speed and bravery for an out-of-shape coward, Sheldon zipped up the ladder like a James Bond trainee. It would have been perfect if he hadn't dropped his spanner just as he reached the top level. The spanner hit every rung on the way down to the concrete deck before rebounding against a stainless steel panel and coming to rest. If a German thrash metal band had started rehearsals inside Dent-O it couldn't have made more noise.

The Brain Finds a Leg

His head just below ceiling level, Sheldon rammed himself against the back wall and tried to melt into the concrete bricks, hoping against hope that somehow the bad guys hadn't heard it.

Of course they had.

Below Sheldon, Fleming and the blond man stood looking at the spanner as if it had materialized from outer space. After a couple of seconds they realized where it had come from. The blond man sprang into action, coming after Sheldon like a greyhound after a rabbit.

"There!" shouted Fleming, pointing his gun at Sheldon. He pulled the trigger and economy-sized chunks of the Dent-O factory exploded out of the walls in a hail of high-velocity bullets.

The bullets thudded into the walls with frightening power. It wasn't like a shoot-out in the movies, thought Sheldon, his legs pounding like pistons as he raced around the gangway. These bullets looked like they could stop a rhino. Sheldon had never liked Fleming but never, not even in his wildest dreams, did he think that one day his homeroom teacher would be chasing him round a toothpaste factory with an automatic weapon.

Below the gangway, The Brain and Feebly were tied to an odd-looking bit of machinery covered in wires and tubes and digital displays. They were being guarded by Horrocks; when he saw Sheldon, he started blazing away too. Great, thought Sheldon, just what I need: another lunatic with a cannon.

"Run!" shouted The Brain. Blood flowed from his mouth, but otherwise he looked in pretty good shape, considering he was being held prisoner by a crazed villain and a cross-dressing former teacher with a gun.

Sheldon didn't need any reminders to keep running, but it was good to get some encouragement. As he neared a corner of the factory, the blond man reached the gangway. He had an even larger gun than Fleming and he wasted no time in using it.

Kapow! A cloud of plaster and cement dust exploded just alongside Sheldon's left ear as he turned the corner. Bullets pinged and clanged everywhere, ricocheting off the metal as Fleming, Horrocks, and the blond man opened up with everything they had—which was plenty. Sheldon dodged and weaved and did his best to take stock of the situation. There was only one conclusion he could reach. It looked bad.

Ahead of him: nothing except more gangway.

Behind him and closing fast: blond man with gun.

Below him: Fleming, also with gun.

Below him, slightly further away and off to one side: Horrocks with yet another gun.

Desperate, Sheldon looked for some place, any place, to hide. A few meters ahead, something caught his eye: an overhead crane, just like the ones that move containers around at seaports. This one ran on a fixed rail along the length of the factory ceiling. Sheldon didn't, as a general rule, have an interest in cranes or heavy machinery. But what interested him particularly in *this* crane was the solid metal cab, which looked as if it might be bulletproof. If he could get to it, there was nothing the gun-toting baddies could do. The crane cab was Safety with a capital *S*.

The only trouble with the crane plan was that the cab window was about two meters away from the edge of the gangway. He would have to make a leap across that gap while bad people fired high numbers of large bullets at him. If he missed, he'd drop straight down to the factory below. Unless Sheldon somehow developed the capacity to fly or catch bullets in his teeth, jumping was the only option.

"He's up by that crane thing!" yelled Feebly from below. "You'll get him if you hurry!"

Sheldon cursed. Why was the twerp trying to ingratiate himself with the bad guys? Everyone who watches movies knows this means you're probably going to be next to cop it. Sheldon sincerely hoped that this would turn out to be true in Feebly's case, but right now hoping was going to get him exactly nowhere.

Sheldon was dimly aware of The Brain cursing Feebly as he gathered what was left of his energy and sprinted for the edge of the gangway. Grunting with the effort, he launched himself into midair, twenty meters above the factory floor. Bullets filled the air (didn't these guys ever run out of ammunition?) and Sheldon thumped into the side of the cab, one arm clinging to a handle. He levered himself up and was just gratefully pulling himself through the open window when he was hit.

It took Sheldon's brain more than a moment to compute the staggering information that he'd been shot. Actually *shot!*

Sheldon, like most people, didn't know anyone who had been shot, or even anyone who *knew* anyone who'd been shot. It wasn't common in Farrago Bay.

Well, Sheldon thought, now I know *exactly* what it feels like to be shot. It hurts. It hurts a lot.

Even though he'd been hit in his rear end, the softest part of his body, it was like being punched by the heavyweight champion of the world wearing gloves coated in ice and hot coals. The bullet knocked him sideways and it was all he could do to cling to the side of the cab.

If you'd asked Sheldon before he'd been shot if it was possible for him to be more terrified than he already was, he'd have laughed. Now he was terrified beyond anything he'd ever experienced: even worse than that time he'd misguidedly borrowed Sean's DVD of *Chainsaw Blood Feast Zombies on the Rampage: Uncut* and watched it by himself late at night.

Screwing his face up tight against the pain, he managed to drag himself through the window of the crane cab. He located the control panel and pressed as many buttons as he could. A hail of bullets smacked into the cab like a cloud of enraged bees. The cab lurched wildly one way, then another, before—fantastically, wonderfully—moving out into the middle of the factory and shuddering to a stop. Sheldon lay panting on the floor of the cab while the bullets bounced harmlessly off the steel, the lovely thick strong steel of the crane cab. Sheldon kissed the floor in gratitude.

He was safe. He was OK.

Apart from the bullet in his bum.

Chapter 23

Sheldon thought about bums. Specifically, he thought about bullets and bums. Bullets were small and heavy and fast. Bums were (mostly) soft and fleshy. In Sheldon's case, having a somewhat well-padded posterior proved to be A Very Good Thing. The bullet had caught him across the edge of one cheek, zipping out the other side in an instant; it left a very painful, but thankfully non-life-threatening streak of blood and ripped skin behind. Sheldon was pleased about the bullet not having connected with any important areas. At least he figured he'd live—for the next few minutes anyway. He took off his camouflage bandanna and, taking it between his teeth, ripped it lengthways to form one long length of cotton. It was none too clean but it would have to do. Feeling slightly silly he dropped his pants and wrapped the bandanna tightly around his buttocks. It wasn't perfect but at least it soaked up some of the blood.

Sheldon pulled his pants back up, hissing through gritted teeth. OK. Time to come up with some cunning plan and rescue the situation. Something really clever, workable and, most of all, *quick,* was what was needed. Unfortunately, it was harder than it looked to come up with a clever plan when there were three homicidal maniacs chasing him with large caliber weapons. Other things kept getting in the way. For example, all Sheldon could think about was his bum. Good ideas came when you were calm, relaxed. And *this* situation was about as far from relaxing as it was possible to be. Sheldon racked his jittery brain for ideas, as he gingerly felt what was left of his rear end.

His hand bumped against something in his pocket. His mother's mobile phone! He'd completely forgotten about it, what with being involved in a gunfight. Sheldon frantically checked the phone for damage. As far as he could see it was OK. Hardly daring to breathe, he flicked open the phone and turned it on. The screen flickered to life and he was in business. The phone had a camera. Maybe, thought Sheldon, if the police didn't believe he was trapped under the ceiling at Dent-O by a pack of gun crazy heavies and a deranged homeroom teacher, the photos would convince them.

The big question was who exactly to call. Sheldon opted, against all his instincts, to call Snook. Snook was, when all was said and done, a policeman. Dumb as a fencepost he might be—and no fan of the McGlones right now—but that didn't mean he wouldn't take this seriously, did it? Did it?

The decision made, Sheldon flipped through the contact list in the phone and found Snook's personal number. As he keyed it in, he risked a peek over the edge of the cab window. Things had quieted down. Maybe they'd all given up? Sheldon raised his eyes to the edge of the window and almost got his hair parted by a couple of nine-millimeter bullets.

So much for that theory.

Rethinking rapidly, Sheldon edged the phone over the rim of the window and clicked away blindly. After a few moments, he pulled it back in and started to check the pictures. Before he could do anything a voice bellowed at him from below. Panicking, Sheldon pressed Send and prayed that there was something, anything in those pictures that would penetrate Snook's thick skull enough to send him and a platoon of cops over to Dent-O ASAP.

"McGlone!" shouted Fleming from the factory floor. "McGlone, we know it's you. You better come out right now, do you hear?"

Sheldon stayed where he was.

"You have two choices, McGlone. One, you stay where you are and we kill your friends. Two, come down and join us and you *may* all survive. No promises, but it's the best offer you're going to get today. You have five seconds."

Jeez.

Talk about a big decision.

"One," said Fleming.

Sheldon started thinking hard.

If he went, that meant they'd have three hostages instead of two, right?

"Two!"

On the other hand, if they killed The Brain and Feebly it'd just be him left alone with these nuts. That wasn't good either.

"Three!"

"Don't do it!" shouted The Brain. "They'll kill you anyway! These ruffians are not going to shoot me just yet."

"Quiet! Four!"

If what The Brain said was true, then it would be Feebly who'd cop it if Sheldon didn't go, and it'd be Sheldon *and* Feebly who'd cop it if he *did* go. The logical decision (if The Brain was right—and from where Sheldon sat that was a pretty big if) was to stay right where he was and take the risk that they were bluffing.

"Five!"

It was now or never. Maybe, Sheldon thought, he should surrender heroically and figure out some way to keep all of them alive. Except that life wasn't like that. Dipstick or not, Feebly didn't deserve to die but if Sheldon had learned anything during this adventure it was that "deserve" didn't come into it. He was sorry about letting Feebly cop it, if that's what it came to, but the dude had made some bad life decisions along the way. Getting gunned down in cold blood by a cross-dressing nut-job homeroom teacher wasn't necessarily the end Feebly deserved, but sometimes stuff happens.

He decided to stay put. Feebly would have to take his chances. Sheldon closed his eyes and waited.

Krak! A single shot echoed through the factory. Then another, and another. Oh my god! thought Sheldon. They'd done it! They'd actually shot Feebly! And it was all Sheldon's fault. What had he done? With a heavy heart Sheldon peeked over the window and saw Feebly still tied to the machine next to The Brain. Alive!

The blond man was shooting at something else.

It was Mavis.

Chapter 24

Mavis wasn't entirely happy. Even from a distance, Sheldon could see that she looked more like a crocodile and less like a Yorkshire terrier. That was one clue. The other was that she was carrying a leg in her mouth. A human leg. Sheldon could see that it wasn't Biff's. He imagined that Biff's leg had long since been guzzled by Mavis, or possibly buried in a back garden like a favorite bone for future consumption. This one looked fresh. It was fully trousered, in blue with yellow piping, and Sheldon had a sneaky suspicion it might have once been attached to the Dent-O security guard last seen heading south down Farrago Road.

Mavis chewed on the leg like a piece of gum and barked in the direction of The Brain. She did this for a few seconds while Fleming, Horrocks, and the blond man watched her warily. Feebly, who'd been goggling at Mavis ever since she'd arrived, moaned softly and fainted.

Sheldon wondered why Mavis had turned up. Then he realized that Mavis had come to show off the new leg, much like she would show off a new stick. It would have been simple for her to follow the sound of gunfire.

"I reckon this thing has got something to do with Four-Eyes here," said Horrocks, looking at The Brain. He waved his gun. "In case you hadn't noticed, you little squirt, we are heavily armed. Croc or no croc, you are still in deep trouble."

He raised his hand and slapped The Brain across the face.

Big mistake.

Sheldon wouldn't have said that Mavis moved like a rocket, exactly, but she raced toward Horrocks faster than anyone would have believed possible if they hadn't seen it for themselves. Spitting out the security guard's leg, she raced across the factory floor and grabbed Horrocks before he knew what had happened.

"*Aiiieeeeeee!!!*" he squealed as she dragged him behind a nearby machine, his gun clattering uselessly to the ground. "Help me!" he wailed at The Brain, his fingers scrabbling on the bare concrete. The Brain shrugged apologetically.

"Sorry, I'd like to help but I'm afraid she's at that awkward puppy stage. Can't do a thing with her. Heel girl! *Heel!* See? Doesn't pay me a bit of notice!"

Horrocks was half in and half out of Mavis's mouth. Fleming and the blond henchman stood gaping, transfixed by the grisly sight.

"What are you waiting for?" Horrocks screamed. "Shoot the bloody thing! Shoot it! Shoo—"

There was a nasty gurgling sound and, before Fleming or the blond man could move, Mavis swallowed the crooked managing director of Dent-O in a few gulps.

Feebly woke up, saw what was happening, vomited all over Fleming's shoes, and passed out once more.

Sheldon took advantage of the shocking scene below him to move the crane into position and then slip into the shadows of the factory. He carefully picked his way along a platform above the big machine to which The Brain and Feebly were tied and huddled amongst a dense tangle of pipes and girders.

Having eaten Horrocks, Mavis burped, yawned, and wandered off, probably to go to sleep. Digesting a slime ball like Horrocks would take it out of anyone.

Fleming turned back to The Brain.

"You think you know everything, don't you?" whispered Fleming savagely.

"The vomit on your shoes somewhat dilutes your evil mastermind persona. As does your fear of being eaten," said The Brain. "Although I think you may rest assured that Mavis will be unconscious for some time; the average saltwater crocodile needs approximately six hours sleep after every large meal."

Fleming pointed the gun at The Brain.

"What makes you so confident I won't kill you?" he spat.

"It is self-evident," said The Brain coolly. "You kidnapped me and the unfortunate Feebly several hours ago, yet here I am still very much alive, if a trifle bloodied. It doesn't take much intelligence to come to the conclusion that you require me for some purpose. Something that requires me to be alive."

"I say we kill him anyway."

Sheldon was surprised that the blond man had spoken. He'd sort of assumed the man was there in a nonspeaking role, an extra in the scenes that needed a bit of muscle. Come to think of it, Sheldon was very surprised that Horrocks had copped it before the blond man. The blond man had "disposable henchman" written all over him. Yet here he was, still standing, which just went to prove that reality wasn't like the movies.

"You may *haff* a point, Konrad," said Fleming. "I am coming around to that point of view myself."

"Fleming," said The Brain, "your accent is slipping."

"My *vhat*—I mean, my what?"

"Your accent. As you have become more agitated, your carefully cultivated Australian tones have begun to ebb, revealing your true geographical origins. To an expert student of regional accents, linguistics, and inflexions, much can be revealed by simple phonetics. Your use of the Germanic *f* as opposed to the Anglo-Saxon *v* centers you in northern Europe. Your word placement indicates a further centralization. Perhaps southern Germany, western Austria...or maybe *Switzerland*?"

Fleming looked at The Brain, eyes wide.

"I would go further," continued The Brain. "I would pinpoint you, based solely on the couple of examples you have revealed in this room, to *Zurich*. Would that be correct, Herr Doktor Dirk P. Unsinn, formerly of the Van Schekling Institute for Cranio-Biological Research?"

Fleming reeled. Sheldon had never really witnessed anyone reeling before, not properly anyway. He'd read about people reeling all the time in various books, but it's not something that happens often in real life, is it?

Fleming was Dr. Dirk Unsinn? Hadn't Unsinn died in that big explosion at the Institute in Zurich?

"But how?" said Fleming. "How could you possibly have known just from a few small *vords*—dammit!— *words*?"

"Oh, I have suspected you for some time, Herr Doktor."

"Not on that first day at the school? That is impossible!"

"No," said The Brain. "Not just at that point, you are quite correct. I *did* realize you were a man, as you know. I think I told you so at the time."

"I could not believe it!" cursed Fleming. "I had had extensive plastic surgery, colored contact lenses—the best money could buy!"

"It was elementary detective work, Herr Doktor. Your hands could not be disguised by surgery. When I handed you that note I noticed they were far too large for a female, even a particularly masculine one. Your feet also were rather large for a woman. And I'd recently undertaken research into male and female voice-modulation patterns for my own amusement. Your word rate was far too slow to be that of a female. I considered the evidence and made the leap. Your reaction confirmed my suspicions."

"Two years!" yelled Fleming. "Two whole years at that cursed school, building my reputation carefully day by day! And then you, *you*, of all people, walk into the classroom! It would be almost funny—if it was not so deadly serious."

"I still say we shoot him now," said the blond man.

"The good Doktor is not yet sure that there isn't some important piece of information about the Genius Machine that I, and I alone possess," said The Brain, looking as calm as you like. "Correct, Doktor?"

Sheldon felt confused. What was all this about a Genius Machine? Wasn't that what The Brain's parents had been working on all those years ago?

"You *knew*?" said Fleming.

The Brain nodded. "The moment I saw it today. Although I had suspected its existence long before I saw it here at Dent-O. It was the teeth, you see. And *The Coreal* disaster."

It was obvious that Fleming did not see. Neither did Sheldon, for that matter. What did *The Coreal* accident have to do with all this?

"The teeth? What are you prattling on about, you idiot?" Fleming said.

"He's stalling, Doktor. Let's shoot him," said the blond man. Had a bit of a one-track mind, he did, thought Sheldon. Once he started talking, you couldn't shut him up.

Or perhaps you could...

Sheldon looked around and saw a girder spanning the roof space right above the blond man and Fleming. If he could somehow get across there and drop something heavy on them... Even to Sheldon it didn't sound like much of a plan, but it was the best he could come up with at short notice. Besides, The Brain seemed to have forgotten that he was still tied up and that Fleming had a gun. If Sheldon didn't do something soon, all The Brain's clever detective work would have been for nothing. It was down to him, Sheldon realized, and him alone. Energized, he looked for something he could use. There! Further along on the gangway was a heavy-looking toolbox left by a careless maintenance worker. Wincing with bum pain, Sheldon inched his way over to the toolkit, picked it up (he was right, the thing weighed a ton), and shuffled to the girder.

"Don't look down," he murmured, stepping out a few paces onto the narrow metal. "Don't. Look. Down."

Chapter 25

Snook picked up the phone on its second ring. "Snook," he snapped. "Hello?" Nothing. It was a text message, not a call.

He checked the caller ID; the message was from Mary McGlone. Snook smiled. The little lady probably wanted to kiss and make up. She couldn't resist the Snookmeister after all. He sat back in the office chair and slicked some spittle across his scalp. She'd sent photos too.

Snook opened the message. What was Mary McGlone doing sending him blurry rubbish like this? He could see what looked like bits of machinery, and he could even see that there were some people in the shot, but that was about it. He pressed a button to see the next photo. This time the image was a little sharper and Snook could see that there were three—no four—people in this shot. It was all so confusing. He looked for more photos in vain before snapping the phone shut.

Snook sat back and wondered what he should do. After a small pause he opened the phone again and pressed "redial."

It was slow, agonizingly slow, but Sheldon was making progress.

Clutching the toolbox with both hands, he straddled the girder. In an awkward, painful half-shuffle, Sheldon scooted over to a point directly above Fleming, who still had the gun trained on The Brain. The blond man stood a little to Fleming's left. Sheldon hoisted the toolbox above his head and took careful aim. This was a one shot deal. Sheldon hoped he could take out the blond man before he shot The Brain. What Fleming would do then was anyone's guess, but Sheldon was hoping that he'd give everything up as a bad job and leave, preferably without shooting anyone. It was a long shot, Sheldon knew, but he was all out of fresh ideas. It was this or nothing.

With a small grunt he hefted the toolbox a little over to the right, his arms trembling with the effort. The bullet wound in his rear throbbed wickedly and Sheldon felt a ripple of dizziness pass through him. Come on Sheldon, he hissed. Do it! Steady, steady, get ready to drop...

The mobile phone in Sheldon's back pocket rang, cutting through the Dent-O factory like a siren in a library. Both Fleming and the blond man automatically swiveled the barrels of their guns toward the sound.

Sheldon dropped the toolbox and was rewarded with the sight of it creaming the blond man smack dab between the eyes. He had no time to savor the sight of the man dropping like a felled tree before Fleming let rip with a volley of bullets. Unbalanced, Sheldon tottered for a second on the edge of the girder and then toppled into space.

They say your life flashes in front of you when you know you are going to die. In Sheldon's case, all that flashed in front of him was the single thought: I don't want to die. No sooner had that registered than he clanged painfully off another girder and bounced head-first right down the throat of the Genius Machine. He remembered The Brain's story about the original explosion in Zurich and hoped that this wasn't going to turn out the same way. For one crazy instant before he clattered his way into the machine, Sheldon could have sworn the air inside the Dent-O factory had filled with smoke and swarms of ninjas were rappelling down through the skylights.

The top of the machine was shaped like a cone. Sheldon slid helplessly around in circles on the stainless steel sides before dropping down into the center. Deep in the machine it was dark; the only light came from the faint green glow of LCD display units. Sheldon banged into hard bits of the interior workings and took a nasty blow to the back of the head. In front of him was what he could only imagine was the dead center of the Genius Machine: a pulsing ball of energy floating in a tank of water. Sheldon splashed down into the water and everything turned white.

Some time had passed. Sheldon was still alive. Boy was he *ever* still alive! He felt *great*! He didn't know where he was or what damage he'd suffered, but Sheldon knew one thing for certain: he'd never felt like this before. It was as if all his senses had been opened up completely, simultaneously. Sheldon looked down at his hand and could see that he'd scraped the subcutaneous epidermis just above the base curve of the ulna, right where the median nerve bisects the transverse carpal ligament. Whoa! How did he know *that*?

Sheldon was still in the Dent-O factory. He lay on his back looking up at the roof (constructed, he couldn't help but notice, by using the Peffhammer and Timble cantilevered bracing system first developed in 1974 by the NASA research team building the first space shuttle prototype). Another thing. The roof was still there, which meant there'd been no explosion.

Of course! Sheldon remembered falling into the Genius Machine. That must be why, he thought, my synaptic neurons were interacting in such an accelerated and highly charged, supersynergetic capacity! Sheldon calculated that his brainpower had increased by a factor of ten. A quick algorithmical quadrilateral biosynthetic cross-referencing memory search told him that he was now officially brainy!

"Snap out of it, Sheldon, my good fellow. Snap out of it, I say!"

The Brain's head came into view. He was alive. He slapped Sheldon's face.

"I'm sorry, old bean, but you are babbling. Now just let me reconfigure these wires…"

The Brain busied himself joining a bundle of wires to a circuit board. Sheldon sat up. The Genius Machine was still intact.

"We haven't blown up!" he said.

The Brain glanced at the machine.

"Of course not. Fleming's version of the machine used none of the explosive elements that my parents had utilized back in the Dark Ages. This machine is virtually indestructible."

"But I don't understand. If the machine didn't fragment under a compressed pressure release, then what mechanism enabled us to evade the inevitability of our demise at the hands of our former educator?"

The Brain looked at Sheldon and shook his head sadly.

"Dear me, old boy, we do need to reverse this Intelligence Boost immediately, don't we? You are beginning to sound like me, and that would never do!"

"But I *like* being intelligent!" Sheldon wailed. "My capacity for pure waves of intelligent thinking is unparalleled in the history of mankind! It would be criminal to withhold the glory of my magnificent brain from the world! I must be allowed to remain, I tell you! I must! Only that way can I lead all of us to the shining path of scientific enlightenment! I—"

Sheldon was cut off mid-rant as The Brain snapped the connectors together. The Genius Machine gave a small burp, shivered for a moment, and then spat out a small white lump of goo into a metal wastebasket attached to its side.

Immediately Sheldon felt everything slow down, as if he'd been watching a speeded-up film that had returned to normal. He sagged. He was back to being Sheldon. It didn't feel good.

"Why did you do that?" Sheldon asked. "I felt...I can't quite think of the word. Begins with an *e*, I think."

"Euphoric?" suggested The Brain.

"That's it! I felt euphoric!"

"That's the problem," said The Brain, clamping his pipe between his teeth.

"Euphoria is but a baby step from lunacy. The important thing is that you're safe! Let's get into town and I'll explain everything."

Chapter 26

A couple of hours later, everyone involved in the case had been rounded up and squeezed into a meeting room at the surf club next to the police station. The station itself, of course, was too small to accommodate everyone and The Pig was full of customers.

Going from left to right around the room were:

Sheldon.

His mother.

Sean.

Feebly, smelling slightly of stale vomit and with an unattractive green tinge to his pasty skin.

Snook, together with the rest of the Farrago Bay police force.

An important-looking man with a thick mustache, wearing a black military-style uniform.

Fleming, who was handcuffed to a chair next to the important-looking man. Still wearing his full woman-suit, Fleming had a bloody gash across his forehead.

A squad of hard-eyed men carrying guns and wearing black military-style uniforms stood to attention against one wall, assault rifles slung across their chests, looking at Fleming coldly.

At the head of the table sat The Brain.

"Gentlemen, ladies, I imagine that some of you may be requiring an explanation of recent events."

Too right, thought Sheldon. A bit of explaining would do very nicely right now, thank you very much. Whatever The Brain had done to reverse his sudden, short-lived flirtation with braininess, it had left Sheldon with a decidedly fuddled head. The group collected in the boardroom did nothing to help that situation. And his bum hurt.

The Brain pointed through the window in the general direction of the Dent-O factory.

"Dent-O is where the explanations for all the events surrounding Biff Manly's death lie. Dent-O is at the center of a web of evil that reaches back across two continents and ten years. It has been responsible for many deaths, including those of my own dear parents and that of Peter McGlone, my good friend Sheldon's father, and three of his passengers on board *The Coreal*. Not to mention the unfortunate Mr. Manly."

There was a gasp from Sheldon's mother, who held her hand to her mouth.

"*The Coreal?*" said Snook. "What in blue blazes has *The Coreal* disaster got to do with a ruddy toothpaste factory?"

The Brain pointed to Fleming.

"It all starts with 'Miss Fleming' arriving in Farrago Bay," he said.

"Miss Fleming?" said Snook, clearly not yet up to full speed.

The Brain stepped across and, for Snook's benefit, pulled off Fleming's wig.

"Let me clarify matters for you, Sergeant. Miss Fleming is, in actual fact, Dr. Dirk P. Unsinn, formerly Director of the Van Schekling Institute for Cranio-Biological Research in Zurich!"

Snook looked like he was going to faint.

"You're a *bloke!*" he gasped.

Sheldon suspected that Snook might have put the make on Fleming at some time in the past.

"So what?" snapped Fleming. "There is no law against wearing woman's clothing!"

Snook didn't look convinced. He looked across to Phil with raised eyebrows. "Isn't there?"

Phil shrugged.

"There may be no law against that," said The Brain. "But there most certainly is against criminal sabotage, industrial espionage, impersonating a school teacher... and *murder!*"

The Brain paused. He had the full attention of every person.

"This saga begins the night when the Genius Machine was first revealed. Consumed by jealousy and greed, Unsinn had plotted to steal the ideas my parents had worked on and use them for his own twisted ends. His initial plan was to simply sabotage the original machine using a small bomb. That way, the demonstration in Zurich would be a disaster, people would forget about the Genius Machine, and, after a short period of time, Unsinn could reintroduce the idea and pass it off as his own. However, there was a problem with his plan."

The Brain paused and took a sip of tea.

"That problem was me. When I fell into the volatile core of the Genius Machine I triggered a much larger explosion than Unsinn had counted on. Instead of simply making the demonstration fail, it destroyed the entire Institute and killed many people. Isn't that right, Dr. Unsinn?"

Miss Fleming/Dr. Unsinn said nothing, but glowered at The Brain.

"No matter," continued The Brain. "Incredible as it may sound, Unsinn survived the explosion. I have a theory; according to the seating plan for the journalists, Unsinn would have been somewhere near a rather large journalist from the *Berlin Times* called Schweinsteiger. It is possible that Schweinsteiger absorbed the worst of the blast."

A black, resentful look from Unsinn confirmed The Brain was right.

"It is, of course, of no importance *how* Unsinn survived; the crucial thing is that he *did* survive and he still had access to my parents' work and plans! There was no one else but him at the Institute who understood the full potential of the Genius Machine. This was his opportunity! Despite his injuries, he escaped the scene of the disaster unobserved, went into hiding, and allowed everyone to think he was dead. Then he formed the deadly scheme which would, he hoped, eventually reach fruition here in Farrago Bay."

Sheldon looked at The Brain. "I don't understand why he came here," he said. "Why Farrago Bay, of all places? Why Australia?"

The Brain paused.

"There were, I believe, several reasons for choosing Farrago Bay. One is that the atmospheric conditions here are ideal for the Genius Machine and for Dr. Unsinn's plans. He needed a very pure water supply for his toothpaste factory. The years between the explosion and Unsinn's arrival in Farrago Bay had been, I think, spent in unsuccessful development of the Genius Machine. It was only perhaps three years ago that Unsinn could finally see exactly what he needed...and that he could find it here in Farrago Bay."

"Wait a minute," said Mrs. McGlone. "What do you mean, *his* toothpaste factory?"

"Dr. Unsinn *owns* Dent-O. Dent-O is a working tooth-paste factory, which masks its true reason for existence—which I will reveal shortly. Now, where was I?"

"Farrago Bay?" said Sheldon.

"Ah yes, thank you, old bean. Unsinn also picked Farrago Bay for two other reasons. Australia is very far away from Unsinn's shadowy past. And Farrago Bay already has so many oddballs that it would be easier for him to blend in. It was also somewhere for him to recover following his latest plastic surgery. His surgeon is only an hour or so up the coast. Unsinn became Miss Fleming and took up work at the local school while he developed his plans; who would ever suspect the spinsterish Miss Fleming of being the mastermind behind this evil scheme?"

Sheldon interrupted.

"Why the surgery?" he said, puzzled. "I mean, who would know him outside Switzerland?"

The Brain pointed to the man with the big mustache. "Let me introduce Captain Schnurrbart of the crack Swiss International Science Brigade Tactical Response Unit, feared throughout the criminal scientific community!"

The captain rose from his seat, nodded to Mrs. McGlone, and saluted, clicking his heels in military fashion. His squad did likewise, the sound echoing around the boardroom.

"Good afternoon, everyone. We have long suspected there might be a reappearance of the Genius Machine. However, our satellite monitoring unit did not begin to pick up indications of odd biological activity in this area until 22 July of the same year that Dent-O began operations at Farrago Bay."

"The day of *The Coreal* disaster!" Sheldon gasped.

"*Ja*," said Captain Schnurrbart, turning toward Sheldon's mother. "*The Coreal* disaster, which deprived this lovely lady of her husband at such a young age. Such a tragic waste."

Sheldon's mother blushed as the captain smiled at her and twiddled the ends of his luxuriant mustache. There was an awkward pause.

"Captain," said The Brain. "Continue."

"Hrmmph. Of course. Where was I? Oh yes, the whales. It was the whales that destroyed *The Coreal*. Humpback whales," said Captain Schnurrbart sadly. "Such gentle, gentle creatures…"

He trailed off, shaking his great mustache, then glared at Unsinn and shot another sympathetic look toward Sheldon's mother.

"We decided several months ago that this area needed looking at more closely," he went on. "We had heard about *The Coreal* when it happened, but, since no further events occurred we waited. Maybe we should have acted sooner...but, to my eternal regret, we didn't. When other activity started a few months ago I talked to Theo"—Captain Schnurrbart nodded toward The Brain—"and brought him here. We inserted him with a host family in Farrago Bay shortly before Mr. Manly's death. His task was to see if there was any evidence that the Genius Machine was in operation. He, after all, was the person with the most intimate knowledge of his parents' work."

"So you're not from Mooloolaba!" blurted Sheldon.

The Brain looked sympathetically at him. "No, Sheldon, I am *not* from Mooloolaba," he said. "That was merely a cover story to account for my presence in the area. My parents in Farrago Bay were actors hired for the mission. It was Nola, in fact, who called Sergeant Snook when she found the crocodile in my room. I had omitted to inform her of Mavis's presence. It was a need-to-know situation."

The Brain turned to Unsinn.

"It was sheer chance that I was assigned to Unsinn's class. Can you imagine his feelings when I walked into the room? I did not recognize him, although, as we know, he clearly knew me by my name. Of course, had we known Unsinn was involved, I would not have used my real name. We assumed he'd died that night at the Institute in Zurich. By turning up in his class I had tipped him off that the Swiss team was onto him."

Sheldon was still confused.

"I'm still confused. How did the SWAT team arrive? Did they already know about Dent-O?"

Captain Schnurrbart, who had by now resumed his seat, took up the story.

"Not at all, Sheldon," he said. "It was just good fortune on our part that our satellite was monitoring all calls in and out of Farrago Bay after Theo had disappeared. One of my operatives picked up the message you sent to Sergeant Snook. We have some GPS software that revealed your location, and it did not take much more information for us to realize the danger that The Brain was in. We organized a cleanup operation as quickly as we could. Although composed entirely of Swiss operatives, the Swiss International Science Brigade Tactical Response Unit is well-known in Australia and around the globe. Your government helped us get into the country—although they would of course deny all involvement should our mission have proved unfounded. The Swiss International Science Brigade Tactical Response Unit does the dirty work that other organizations cannot!'

The Brain looked slowly around the room, tapped his pipe against his teeth, and continued. He looked like he was enjoying himself.

"Dent-O started production in Farrago Bay around the same time as *The Coreal* disaster. That was the first sign of things to come, the first sign that something in this area was altering the behavior of the animals. Unsinn had recruited a man called Len Wimslow, who you all knew as Horrocks, to act as the front man and all-round muscle at Dent-O. Mr. Wimslow, as you know, is no longer with us."

The Brain pointed outside toward the car park where Mavis slept under a tree, a look of contentment on her face. A shoelace snaked out from between two of her white teeth.

"So Dent-O was just a cover?" asked Sheldon.

"Not quite, my dear fellow, not quite. Dent-O is a fully functioning and highly successful factory that supplies toothpaste around Australia daily. It was important as cover for the Genius Machine, but it was equally important for the next stage of Unsinn's plan, which was to distribute a chemical product from the Genius Machine via the toothpaste. Unsinn's plan was to send out supplies of Dent-O Gleem toothpaste to every household in Australia. There was one small, important, and diabolical difference to this toothpaste. Unsinn had changed its molecular structure by reversing the coding of the chemical produced by the Genius Machine. Instead of making people clever, this chemical made people stupid. Once they started using Dent-O toothpaste, Australians would have become a nation of cretins within six weeks. If Dent-O could corner the toothpaste market with aggressive advertising and cut-price offers, then only those with bad dental hygiene would be safe. Unsinn calculated that they did not matter."

"They do *not* matter!" yelped Unsinn. "Who ever listens to anyone with bad teeth? Pah!"

Sean scratched his head, his handcuffs clinking. Snook was still not sure what was going on and, until he was, Sean was still murder suspect Number One.

"Dude, I still don't see where Manly came into it. Or me for that matter," said Sean.

"It was the water," said The Brain. "The Dent-O factory discharges its run-off water into the creek, which in turn runs into the ocean. The animals in the area who drank from the creek or who swam in its water— even when it reached the ocean—all became highly evolved, very quickly. That is why the humpbacks crushed *The Coreal*. When Unsinn heard about *The Coreal*, he changed production back to normal toothpaste. He was scared that if the Swiss heard about what had happened, they would put two and two together and investigate. Which, as the captain has explained, is very nearly what *did* happen. For two years the toothpaste was produced in the normal way. Unsinn only began illegally discharging the run-off water again after he made changes that he thought *wouldn't* affect the sea life (and therefore attract unwanted attention). The only problem is that he was wrong: the marine life was not affected, but those animals who drank from the creek or ate plants with roots in the creek, *were*."

Sheldon could hardly breathe. So *that* was what had happened to *The Coreal!* It wasn't his dad's fault at all! He felt a weight lifting from his shoulders. Of course, knowing what had happened wouldn't bring his father back. He glared at Unsinn with renewed venom.

The Brain looked at Sheldon sympathetically before continuing.

"For some reason, the toothpaste chemicals had the opposite effect on animals. Instead of making them stupid, it increased their intelligence. The polluted whales saw that by acting together, they could be more power-ful. This was also the case with the koalas who killed Mr. Manly."

"*Koalas?*" Snook looked as shocked as if The Brain had accused the Australian cricket team of taking a bribe.

"Koalas," nodded The Brain. "Normally shy and retiring tree-dwellers, the koalas, with increased intel-ligence capacity, organized themselves into a formida-ble hunting pack. Humans were the obvious target. Even though koalas derive much of their fluid intake from the water contained in leaves, they must have consumed enough of the toxins to alter their natural behavior. Mr. Manly simply strayed into their territory at the wrong time. An examination of his leg showed me that it had received a large number of small bites. A comparison with the bite radius of the koala was quite easy to make. Your coroner, the capable Annie Madison, would have had no inkling that koalas would do this, so she never contemplated such tests. She also could not have known of Mavis's presence in the area, which was why she could not pinpoint how Manly's leg had been removed. Meanwhile, Unsinn was growing nervous. When he heard about Manly's death, he was afraid that an investigation might lead back to Dent-O. He instructed Horrocks to find a likely suspect—in this case Sean—and make sure that Sergeant Snook had all the evidence he needed: wit-nesses, DNA, and so forth. What Unsinn had not counted on was my appearance in Farrago Bay. That was when his scheme began to unravel. It must have been a dreadful shock for him when I walked into his classroom."

The Brain sucked his unlit pipe thoughtfully.

"Of course, there is the also the question of Mavis. As you know, she is a saltwater crocodile who is many miles south of her normal habitat. That fact alone threw me off the scent for a long time. It seemed to have no relation to the other examples of animal behavior. A change in the Farrago Bay water supply would not explain why this crocodile was so far south. Faced with the evidence available, I consider there to be only one likely explanation: Mavis is a discarded pet who had outgrown the home she was in. This theory may also explain why, when she increased in intelligence, she imitated the actions of a family dog. Observe also her remarkably white, healthy teeth: clear evidence of fluoride and other dental material in the run-off water from the factory. Farrago Bay, as you may be aware from the number of rotten teeth in this area, does not use fluoride in its water supply. That alone should have told me the answer lay at Dent-O. If there was no fluoride in the town water supply, it must have been coming from the water run-off from Dent-O!"

"The kangaroos?" said Sheldon. "And all the rest of the weird animal stuff? Did they all drink the water?"

The Brain nodded.

"Yes, Sheldon, and these animals were not the only ones exhibiting behavior changes. There have been other events occurring with increasing frequency as the dosage increased. I have noted several examples of lorikeet, possum, and horse behavior that are directly related to this case."

"One thing still puzzles me," said Sheldon.

"Yes?"

"Why did they need you? I mean, why did they kidnap you? And then, having kidnapped you, why didn't they just, you know, kill you?"

"A good question. The short answer is that when I turned up in Farrago Bay Unsinn did indeed panic. His initial thought, I have no doubt, was to kill me. Having reflected on the matter, he decided to keep me alive in case I could be useful. After all, it *was* my parents who had built the original Genius Machine, and I *had* fallen inside that machine. Unsinn was still uncertain that the Genius Machine was working well enough. He had had a setback with the whale incident and he could see from the animal behavior that those problems were still around. I think he planned to get everything he could from me about the Genius Machine, clear up the mess that resulted from Biff Manly's death, and *then* kill me. It had taken him almost ten years to get the machine ready for production, so my arrival was a double-edged sword: I was obviously a threat that must be dealt with, but I could conceivably also be useful. That's what kept me alive, I have no doubt.

"I sent Unsinn a note suggesting I knew all and was about to reveal it to Sergeant Snook. They—Horrocks and Konrad, his blond sidekick, under instruction from Unsinn—took the bait, followed me to The Pig. The rest is history."

"You *wanted* to be kidnapped?" said Sheldon. "But why?"

"I knew that my best chance of getting to the heart of the case was to flush out whoever was behind the whole thing. Remember that until I was kidnapped I did not know that Fleming was Unsinn. I did have some suspicions, but my firm belief that Unsinn was long dead meant that I had to take risks. I knew that Horrocks was merely a front, but I was after the bigger fish. I relied on your abilities to bring events to a head."

"But what if I hadn't found you?" Sheldon asked. "What would have happened then?"

"You *did* find me. I considered your skills to be sufficient to track me to Dent-O and I also considered that Captain Schnurrbart would be monitoring the area for unusual activity—which you provided in abundance, old bean."

"We almost did it!" screeched Unsinn. "If it hadn't been for you meddling teenagers I would have got clean away with it!"

Sheldon almost burst out laughing. No one, surely, in the history of bad guys, had ever actually said that, had they?

There was a pause.

"So what happens now?" Sheldon asked.

"Dr. Unsinn will be returned to Switzerland to face the Swiss Science Courts," said Captain Schnurrbart, a dark smile on his face.

"Nooooo!" howled Unsinn. He turned to Snook. "Sergeant, beat me, throw me in jail for as long as you like! Anything, I implore you, *anything* but the Swiss Science Courts!"

"You got a flaming cheek, Miss Fleming—I mean, whatever your name is," said Snook, his face reddening. "When I think of that night at the Police Ball when I asked you to dance..."

Everyone glanced sideways at everyone else. There was an awkward moment until the Swiss International Science Brigade Tactical Response Unit hauled Unsinn up and out of the room. Captain Schnurrbart stood, then bent down and kissed Sheldon's mother's hand.

"I will see to it personally that this wretch receives the maximum possible punishment. You have my word as an officer. *Und* perhaps you would do me the great honor of taking coffee with me before I leave for Switzerland?"

Sheldon's mother nodded, her mouth open. Snook glowered at Captain Schnurrbart.

Captain Schnurrbart nodded to the room.

"Gentlemen," he said and saluted.

With that he clicked his heels once more and was gone.

Snook let out a long sigh. He nodded at Sean, and Phil released Sean's handcuffs.

It was all over.

The Bit at the End...

Sheldon could hardly believe the adventure had finished. They had actually done it—they had solved Biff Manly's murder and saved Sean. In the process they had uncovered a dastardly plot to turn Australia (and possibly the entire planet) into idiots. Not to mention that they had discovered, finally, more or less what had happened to *The Coreal.* And that, Sheldon decided, was probably the one thing that he was most pleased about. It *hadn't* been his dad's fault. All those snide little whispers and wisecracks had been silenced once and for all.

Sean replaced Biff Manly as the Dent-O sponsored surfer, got a new haircut, moved into his own flat, and never completely understood what had happened. Sheldon tried to explain but it wasn't easy. Sheldon wondered if The Brain could put Sean in the Genius Machine, but it had been destroyed by the Swiss after discussions with The Brain.

After seeing how the Genius Machine had affected the animals, The Brain agreed that people would probably be better off remaining as dumb as they normally were. The machine was reduced to rubble in a top-secret controlled explosion one night.

Dent-O itself remained open. A company that didn't pour weird intelligence-fluid into the creek had bought the factory. It increased production and employed three hundred of Farrago Bay's residents, all of whom now had slightly whiter smiles...but weren't any more intelligent than they used to be.

Mavis made a full recovery and was taken north to a zoo near Darwin where they *liked* crocodiles, the bigger the better. She gradually forgot all about being a dog, although she still enjoyed chasing sticks when given the chance. She spent her time eating chickens and performing staged stunts at Kaptain Krocodile's Koala and Kroc Sanctuary in Port Moreleigh.

Of the killer koalas there had been no sign around Farrago. However, there were reports of a series of muggings from towns up and down the east coast. Witnesses who reported the assailants as being short and hairy with bulbous black noses were, frankly, disbelieved. The Brain said that the muggings would most likely stop when the effects of the polluted water wore off.

The thieving kangaroos and car-jacking possums did not reoffend (as far as anyone could tell). The whales passed through as usual, although whale-watching bookings had not recovered to the levels they were at before *The Coreal* sinking.

Horrocks's funeral was a quick, thinly attended affair. Most people felt that the sooner he was below ground, the better for all concerned. Of course, it was an almost empty casket, as very little of Horrocks had been recovered and it wasn't thought right to bury a pile of crocodile poop, no matter how much of it was Horrocks.

Mungo Mushkin, the unlucky Dent-O security guard, survived the attack by Mavis, although with one leg fewer than he started out with. However, during his stay at Farrago Bay hospital he met and married one of the nurses, so Mungo considered he'd come out of the deal pretty well.

Carefree O'Toole gave up pet psychiatry. After being chipped free of the lorikeet guano pile he seemed to lose interest in animal welfare and became mayor of Farrago Bay.

Bren and Bret were crushed to death a week after the shoot-out at Dent-O when one of their building projects in Maroochydore collapsed during a council inspection. Fortunately they were the only casualties.

Smudger the horse still lives in the paddock opposite The Pig in a Poke. The horse has stopped hunting sparrows.

By all that's fair, Sheldon figured, Unsinn should have died one of those grisly deaths. He *was*, after all, the one who started all this nonsense in the first place. Plus, during the last two years as Sheldon's evil transvestite English teacher, he had made Sheldon's life a living hell.

Yet he did manage to stay alive, and he was being reeducated at the notorious Swiss Science Ministry just outside Lucerne in Switzerland. Part of the therapy involved listening to wholesome family musicals for months on end, so Sheldon supposed that was almost punishment enough.

Snook resumed his job as sergeant. Sheldon had briefly worried that his mother would forgive and forget that he'd stitched up Sean, and take Snook back, but it didn't happen. Never cross a McGlone woman, she'd said—they keep grudges.

In any case, before the Swiss SWAT team left, she saw quite a bit of Captain Schnurrbart. So much, in fact, that, after a whirlwind romance, Sheldon's mother married the captain (and his mustache) in a touching ceremony on Lookout Point. Which made the captain Sheldon's stepfather, which was kind of weird. It turned out that Captain Schnurrbart was The Brain's legal guardian, so Sheldon and The Brain were now officially brothers. And, of all the strange things that happened in Farrago Bay, that was perhaps the strangest, reflected Sheldon.

The Brain and Sheldon settled back comfortably in their first-class seats, drinks in hand. In front of them, the new Mrs. Schnurrbart fondly fondled the captain's mustache. The family was on their way to live in Switzerland. *Switzerland!* Sheldon could hardly believe it. He didn't really know where Switzerland was, or what it looked like, or what language they spoke, or anything.

"Swiss Air would like to welcome passengers to this

flight to Zurich via Singapore. Our journey time will be approximately nine hours to Singapore..."

Sheldon tuned out the announcement and looked at Australia slipping along underneath the plane. Who knew how long it would be before he saw it again? His brand new brother tapped him on the arm.

"Regrets, old boy?" said The Brain, twirling his glass thoughtfully. "Leaving the old country behind?"

Sheldon thought for a moment. He'd never set foot outside Australia before, but then again, before meeting The Brain, he'd never thrown sticks for a crocodile, inspected a surfer's leg, investigated an evil toothpaste murderer, dropped a toolbox on a gun-toting hench-man, or been shot in the bum.

"I think I'll take my chances."

They clinked glasses, adjusted their TV sets, and set-tled back for the long journey.

What's next for Sheldon and The Brain? Find out in

The Brain Full of Holes

The Brain adjusted his battered spectacles, lifted the corner of his identical sandwich with the end of his unlit pipe, and peered suspiciously inside. "Remarkable," he said.

"I know!" said Sheldon shaking his head from side to side. "Swiss cheese. Again!"

"Ah," said The Brain. "That wasn't quite what... never mind."

The Brain was always doing things like that. Just when you thought you knew what he was thinking, he'd surprise you by revealing that he was, in fact, thinking about something entirely different.

Sheldon had almost finished his sandwich.

"You know, if this was a book, someone would pop up and explain exactly how we got here."

"Hmm?" said The Brain absentmindedly. His attention still seemed to be on the contents of the Swiss cheese sandwich.

"I said, if this was a book, someone would tell everyone about us solving the case back in Farrago Bay..."

"Yes, old boy," said The Brain, "*if* this was a book, that would almost certainly be the case, but I'm afraid real life's not like that. Fascinating as it is, the story of how we thwarted the evil machinations of the wicked Dr. Dirk Unsinn will have to remain our secret. No-one will 'pop up,' as you say."

"I suppose you're right," said Sheldon.

Sheldon concentrated on his sandwich, then realized that The Brain was speaking again. "What? Hmm?" said Sheldon.

"The cheese sandwiches, dear boy."

"What about the cheese sandwiches?"

Was The Brain still droning on about those cheese sandwiches? Sometimes he was like a dog with a bone.

"Holes," said The Brain. "That's what about them."

Sheldon shrugged. "So what?" he said. "Swiss cheese is full of holes. That's the whole point of Swiss cheese. Hey? Did you see what I did there? You said *holes* and I said *whole*—"

"Yes, very good, Sheldon. Most amusing."

"Don't sulk," said Sheldon. "What were you saying about the holes?"

"They've gone," said The Brain.

"Gone? What do you mean 'gone?' A hole isn't really there in the first place, is it? How can it go?"

"Observe," said The Brain, opening his sandwich and thrusting it under Sheldon's nose. "My sandwich has cheese, as you can see. Plenty of cheese, in fact. A positive abundance of the stuff. Rather more than I prefer, to be perfectly honest. But as must be plain, there is a complete absence of holes. An absence of absences, you might say. Of my holes there is no sign. *Rien de* holes. *Keine* holes."

The Brain was right.

The holes had completely disappeared.

Still, they *were* just holes. Sheldon found that he just couldn't work up very much excitement about their disappearance.

"Holes, shmoles, what does it matter? Probably just a dud batch of cheese Mum used or something. Who cares?"

The Brain paused. "You do not think it is of interest, this lack of holes? In my humble opinion, this is a most singular occurrence and one that I am determined to investigate until I am satisfied with the outcome. As far as this being a dud batch, I can assure you of this: the cheese from which this particular sandwich has been made was placed in the refrigerator yesterday evening. I observed that it had, at that time, a full complement of holes. That, dear boy, is why the current hole-free situation is so deuced odd."

Sheldon looked at his own sandwich with more interest. If what The Brain said was true, then it *was* a bit odd that the holes had somehow disappeared overnight. He peeled back the top layer of bread and checked his own sandwich.

No holes.

"Couldn't it just be a coincidence?" said Sheldon. "Maybe Mum switched cheeses last night after we went to bed?"

The Brain nodded. Sheldon could tell it was the sort of nod that, when translated, meant "I'm nodding, but not because I agree with you, but to suggest that you are, in fact, an idiot."

Sheldon gave up. Trying to figure out what The Brain was talking about often made his head hurt. He picked up his can of Floop, the repulsive home-brand version of Coke that his mother insisted on buying, and took a slurp.

"Typical," he said, looking at the can in disgust. "Flat as a pancake."

The Brain looked up, his eyes bright.

"Flat, you say? May I?"

Sheldon reluctantly handed him the Floop. Flat or not, it was still the only one he had.

The Brain took a pull on the can and screwed up his face.

"A truly nauseating concoction. But you are correct, it is quite devoid of carbonation."

Sheldon looked blank.

"No bubbles," explained The Brain. "Interesting."

Sheldon grabbed back the can and drained it in one greedy gulp.

"Yeah," he said, burping. "Very interesting. You got any more Floop? One with bubbles?"

The Brain poured steaming Earl Grey tea from a silver thermos into the monogrammed, fine bone-china teacup he brought to school every day.

"Good grief, no," he said, stirring the tea with a gleaming silver teaspoon. "One has one's standards, old boy."

He sipped his tea thoughtfully, picked up his sandwich once again and inspected it closely.

Sheldon shook his head sadly. The Brain was a certified genius (he had the certificate on his bedroom wall to prove it), but sometimes Sheldon had to wonder if his stepbrother was, perhaps, a few sandwiches short of the full picnic. Even if they were Swiss cheese sandwiches.

Holes or no holes, bubbles or no bubbles, there seemed to be little chance of solving the puzzle this lunchtime. Once that bell sounded for the afternoon, class work started immediately. This was Switzerland after all.

Sheldon grabbed The Brain's sandwich.

"If you're not going to eat that, do you mind if I have it? Thanks." Without waiting for a reply, he crammed it into his mouth.

"Stop!" yelled The Brain. "You're eating the evidence!"